MAGIC

WHITE HAVEN WITCHES (BOOK 2)

UNBOUND

TJ GREEN

Magic Unbound
Mountolive Publishing
Copyright © 2019 TJ Green
All rights reserved
ISBN978-0-9951163-3-7

Other Titles by TJ Green

Tom's Arthurian Legacy Series
Excalibur Rises - Short Story Prequel
Tom's Inheritance
Twice Born
Galatine's Curse
Tom's Arthurian Legacy Box Set

White Haven Witches Series
Buried Magic

Invite from the author -

You can get two free short stories, *Excalibur Rises* and *Jack's Encounter*, by subscribing to my newsletter. You will also receive free character sheets of all the main Whitehaven Witches.

By staying on my mailing list you'll receive free excerpts of my new books, as well as short stories, news of giveaways, and a chance to join my launch team. I'll also be sharing information about other books in this genre you might enjoy.

Details can be found at the end of *Magic Unbound*.

Cast of Characters

Avery Hamilton - descended from Helena Marchmont
Alex Bonneville - descended from Imogen Bonneville
Gil Jackson - descended from Garrett Jackson
Reuben Jackson - descended from Garrett Jackson
Elspeth Robinson - descended from Rowena Kershaw
Briar Ashworth - descended from Raleigh Ashworth
Mathias Newton - descended from Peter Newton
Caspian Faversham - descended from Thaddeus Faversham

1

Avery waited impatiently outside the Witch Museum. It was 2:30 in the morning, and the small town of White Haven was quiet, other than the sound of unearthly grunts and snarls that came from inside the building. The devil's trap had caught something, and the warning she had set up had triggered, waking her from a fitful night's sleep. Any minute now, the other witches would arrive.

It was Sunday night, three nights after Gil's death, and Avery felt gritty-eyed and sleep deprived. If she was honest, she was happy to be woken by the need to do something useful. His death had left her tossing and turning, pondering what-ifs and maybes. She hadn't seen the others since then.

Avery glanced nervously around the car park. If that was a demon in the museum, and it certainly sounded like one, someone had summoned it. If it was Faversham, and she was convinced it must be, was he close by, or doing this from a distance?

As she looked towards the town, she saw shadows edge across the car park. It was the other witches, and she sighed with relief.

Alex blinked back tiredness. "How long?"

"Thirty minutes at most," she said, adjusting her backpack with her grimoire in it.

Briar nodded in acknowledgement. "I can't believe the trap worked. I've got goose bumps." She looked around. "No Reuben?"

Avery shook her head. "No. I didn't think we should disturb him. Have you seen him, El?"

"No. He doesn't want to see anyone right now." El seemed like she was trying to sound cool about it, but Avery detected a tightness in her voice that wasn't normally there.

"Fair enough," Alex nodded. "Let's get on with it. I've brought my new grimoire—there's a spell that I think will work."

"Excellent," Avery said, "because my idea feels shaky. And guys, someone must have summoned that demon. They may still be here." She turned to the back door and with a whispered spell, the door unlocked and they slipped into the museum.

The smell of blood and mustiness was heavy in the air, but stronger than that was the scent of sulphur. The noise in here was louder, too, and her skin pricked at the feral, inhuman sounds that came from inside the main room. A flickering orange light illuminated the doorway.

"What's causing that?" El whispered.

"We'll soon find out," Alex said, leading the way.

A shudder ran down Avery's spine as she saw the dark, multi-limbed, writhing shape, bursting against the constraints of the devil's trap. As the demon saw them enter the room, it howled, revealing a large mouth filled with sharp teeth, and its blood red eyes fixed them with a piercing stare. On the wall behind it was the occult doorway that it had travelled through. The sigils were alight with flames, and acrid smoke poured off them; Avery could see indistinct shapes lurking in the other dimension.

"May the Great Goddess protect us," Briar whispered. She stood, making her personal preparations that Avery was slowly becoming familiar with. She removed her shoes and stood barefoot, grounding herself ready to draw the Earth's strength.

Alex pulled his grimoire free and set it up on a small display case, working quickly and surely, while El pulled a short sword out of her pack and stood poised, ready to strike.

Avery watched them with interest. "What's with the sword, El?"

"After you used the ceremonial sword successfully the other night to help you channel air, I thought I would bind this one with fire—it's smaller and easier to carry, and there's a little something extra in there, too." She grinned at Avery. "Fun times."

"Well, that's one way of putting it."

"Alex, if your banishing spells don't work, what's the back-up plan?" El asked.

"A shit-storm of elemental magic?" Alex looked at them and grinned. "I've got this. Trust me. Just give me one more minute."

Avery took deep, calming breaths and tried to focus. Magic worked best with a clear head and a definite plan. While she waited for Alex, Avery watched the demon. The last time they had encountered them, she had fought them so quickly it had been impossible to study them properly, but now that this one was trapped, she could take her time. Like the other demons, it was made of fire and smoke, its form threatening but seemingly insubstantial. However, this one was bigger, with more limbs. Power radiated from it. It writhed so quickly, it was difficult to make out its complete form, or if it even had one. It seemed to constantly shift, one limb morphing into another, and its eyes moved around within what she assumed was its head. It snapped its huge, gaping mouth, revealing long, sharp teeth, and its growls of frustration were like hearing nails scraped down a blackboard. Fire whips struck against the invisible trap's walls, desperately trying to reach them.

Behind it, the occult doorway was fascinating, fire blazing across its runes and sigils. She wondered if the trapped demon meant the doorway couldn't close.

Alex shouted, "I'm ready! Repeat after me."

They linked hands and Alex started his spell. It was written in archaic English, and at first he stumbled over the words, but then he became more confident and they repeated the words together, each cycle growing in power and conviction.

The demon writhed even more furiously, its shape changing too quickly to register. Avery almost stepped back, its ferocity was so scary, but she held her ground and raised her voice, finding strength in its desperate attempts to escape.

Then, with an almighty crack, the invisible walls of the devil's trap shattered and a rope of flames streaked across the room, whipped around Briar's ankle, and pulled her towards the doorway. It seemed the trap still had some power as the demon stayed within its circle, but more and more flame ropes lashed towards them.

Briar slithered across the floor screaming and trying to break free, hurling energy bolts at the demon, but it was too strong.

El loosed Avery's hand and ran across the room, wielding her sword that now flashed with a white flame.

Avery wavered for a moment, but Alex tightened his grip on her hand, repeating the spell, and she drew on her power once again, binding her strength with his as they repeated the words faster and faster.

Elspeth sliced and hacked at the flame ropes, moving with athletic fury. The ropes shrivelled as she cut them, but she still couldn't get to Briar who was being pulled closer and closer to the demon. She renewed her attack, and Avery tried not to lose concentration. Finally Elspeth sliced through the flame rope holding Briar, just as she reached the edge of the trap.

With an insidious whisper, the doorway changed and they all almost faltered. Avery had thought it was open before, but as their spell started to work, the runes faded away, revealing the dimension in all its horror. It was like staring into a gigantic whirlpool of fire that stretched back aeons—it was time that Avery sensed, not space, and it was terrifying.

El grabbed Briar and hauled her across the room, both of them stumbling in their haste.

But the doorway was open for mere seconds. It sucked the demon back within its realms and the doorway shut with a resounding roar, plunging them into darkness.

For a second no one moved, and then Avery spelled a ball of witch light into her hands and threw it up towards the ceiling where it floated, illuminating the space below.

"Everyone okay?" Avery asked. Her heart pounded in her chest, and she felt a little dizzy.

Alex stood immobile, and then he grinned. "Hell yeah! I just banished a demon and closed a dimension—don't thank me all at once!"

"I meant El and Briar," she said with a raised eyebrow. "But well done. It was very impressive."

"Impressive? It was bloody awesome!"

Avery grinned and winked at him. "Only kidding. It's interesting that your grimoire has such spells."

Briar interrupted them. "Don't worry about us—I only almost got sucked into some infernal dimension. El, thank you. You were brilliant." Briar looked pale, and she held her hands over her ankle and calf for a few seconds, murmuring a spell. "That really hurts. It would have been a lot worse without my jeans on."

El smiled and looked at her sword. "This worked better than I thought."

"So what was your special something in the sword?" Avery asked.

"Ice fire."

"Is that even a thing?"

"It is now. Demons don't like it."

"Wow. This night is so weird."

Alex stepped closer to the closed occult doorway, pulling a large potion bottle out of his pocket. "One final thing." He opened the bottle and threw the contents over the doorway with a final incantation, and the runes and marks started to fade until they completely disappeared. "Done. Nothing's coming out of that again."

El looked puzzled. "But who summoned the demon? Where are they?"

Alex shrugged. "Maybe it was done from a distance. Wherever they are, they were trying to disrupt White Haven."

"Maybe it's a distraction," Avery suggested.

"From what?" El asked. "We've protected everything we can."

Briar stood and joined them. "Maybe whoever did this thought the demon would kill one of us. We're too good. I finally feel like we have a win."

"Come on," Alex said. "Let's clean up this place and get out of here."

"Wait," Avery said, moving towards the shattered display next to where the doorway had been. It hadn't been changed since the night they were last here. Underneath the broken glass was a simple ink line drawing depicting Helena, tied to the stake. She was wrapped in a cloak, and her dark hair was flying around her face as if a strong wind was blowing. A man leant forward with a burning branch to light the pyre beneath. Around the pyre, a group of people watched. Avery shuddered. *Poor Helena.* She thought back to their interview with Samuel Kingston. *What if she had been betrayed?* Avery had to find out.

Next to the picture was a display of objects used on an altar. There was an Athame, ancient and worn, its blade dull, the hilt patterned with an old Celtic design. Next to it was an engraved chalice, a ritual bowl made of silver, and two pillar candles that had once been lit. There were two dishes made out of carved wood, the traces of what Avery presumed was salt in one, the other traditionally used for water. The objects were laid out symmetrically on a white cotton cloth, all sealed within a glass-framed display case. Bundles of plants were lined up at the back of the altar, and Avery recognised bay leaves, rowan berries, acorns, oak leaves, and a spiral of hazel branches. She smiled, realising that it really was an altar, placed here many years ago, Helena watching over it.

An old leather book lay to the side, filled with pages of writing. It looked like a ledger, and underneath it was a sign that read: *"Final sales records from Helena Marchmont's business."* Avery flicked through the pages with avid curiosity. *Had this been written by Helena's own hand?* As the witch light glowed from above, a silvery shape began to appear on the open pages in the centre of the book. Avery gasped. It was a message.

No, it was a map.

She reached forward, brushing away shards of glass and reached in for the book.

"What's up, Avery?" Alex asked, coming to stand next to her.

"Look!" She lifted the book and turned it under the light. "It's a map."

He leaned in closer. "A map! Of what?"

She shook her head. "I don't know."

El and Briar joined them, Briar smiling. "This has been here all these years, waiting for you to find it."

"Could it show us where her grimoire is?" Alex asked.

"What else could it be?"

For the first time in days, Avery felt a spark of excitement run through her. After Gil's death, nothing had seemed worth it. Even banishing the demon and closing the doorway, although important, had weighed upon her shoulders. She had questioned what they were doing, and wondered if it was worth the risk. But it had to be. The path to her grimoire was right in front of her.

2

The day of Gil's funeral was overcast and gusty, which was exactly how it should be, Avery thought.

It was Thursday, a whole week since Gil's death, and the days in between had felt long and incredibly sad. Other than needing to banish a demon, nothing out of the ordinary had happened. Avery was grateful for the respite, but it was unnerving. She was on edge, waiting for something to happen while trying to get on with life. She presumed Faversham had summoned the demon, but if he had, he hadn't waited to attack them, and their homes were intact once they returned. Maybe El was right and they had injured him during their battle in the smugglers' tunnels. Well, it wouldn't last long. He would heal quickly, and their brief respite would be over all too soon.

The shock of Gil's death had resonated through the town and it seemed the whole of White Haven was attending the funeral, which was taking place at Old Haven Church, perched on a cliff top overlooking the sea. It had stood there weathering wind, rain, and sun since the 12th century, and the cemetery was snuggled around it, crouched beneath gnarled trees misshapen by the wind. The church was made of huge blocks of stone and had a solid square tower. It was one of several churches in White Haven, and no one was buried there anymore—the plots were full. Only Gil's family status and the fact that they had a mausoleum had allowed for that.

As Avery exited the church after the short service that extolled Gil's virtues without making any mention of his pagan beliefs, she looked around at the grounds, wondering if some of her family might be buried here. They may be witches, but they still ended up in a cemetery like everyone else.

Briar sniffed into a tissue next to her, and Avery put an arm around her shoulder. "Are you all right, Briar?"

"Not really. I think I might start sobbing soon, and then I'd be really embarrassed."

"You and me both, then," Avery said, as she stepped to the side of the path, pulling Briar with her.

Alex and Reuben were two of the pallbearers, along with three of Gil's close friends from the business, and a distant cousin. They exited the church, leading the way down the path to the mausoleum a short distance away under a broad, shady tree. They all looked smart in dark, single-breasted suits, and Avery couldn't help but smile. She'd never imagined she'd see either Alex or Reuben in a suit. Reuben looked a million miles away, his expression grim, and he stared into the distance, seeming to barely register anyone.

Most of the town peeled away after the service, probably heading to the pub where the wake was being held, but El joined Avery and Briar, her eyes red and puffy. She had been sitting at the front with Reuben, and Avery gave her a wan smile as they followed behind Alicia, Gil's widow, who walked with her parents and a few close friends.

Alicia was a petite blonde with sharp blue eyes, and she wore a smart black suit. Avery had met her a few times, but didn't really know her well, and the only thing she had said to her all day was, "I'm so sorry, Alicia. If you need anything..."

Alicia had merely nodded, her eyes red, and Avery couldn't work out if she was furious with her for being part

14

of the events that led to Gil's death, or if she was just in mourning. Or acting. She still suspected her of being a spy for Faversham.

Avery nodded in greeting to a few of the mourners who were joining them at the mausoleum and then slowed down so that they were far enough behind that they couldn't hear. She quietly asked El, "How's Alicia doing?"

El shrugged. "I honestly don't know. She's polite, but that's all. She's barely spoken to me, but I don't see much of her, so why should she?"

Avery nodded and kept her thoughts to herself. She told no one of her fears other than Alex, and they had barely seen each other over the past week, except for the night at the Witch Museum.

"And what about Reuben? How's he doing?"

El dropped her head, silent for a moment, before looking at Avery and Briar. "He can barely look at me, never mind speak to me. I think he blames me."

"You don't know that," Avery said, trying to comfort her. "He's grieving and angry. He'll come round."

"I've never seen him like this before. Whatever we had is gone."

Briar hugged her. "It will be okay. It will just take time."

The mausoleum came into view. It was an ornate stone building with a pitched roof, a double door made from thick wooden planks, and an enormous keyhole. Avery shuddered. It wasn't somewhere she would like to spend eternity. She'd rather be buried beneath a tree or cremated and scattered amongst her plants.

At the entrance the vicar said a few words, most of them lost on the wind, and the pallbearers carried the coffin inside.

The wind seemed to howl in this spot and the leaves above them rustled furiously, some of them flying loose and swirling around them. Avery looked around cautiously. She wouldn't put it past Faversham to be standing by and gloating somewhere in the periphery, but the only person now in sight was DI Newton, stepping between the trees and tombstones to reach them.

Avery nudged El and Briar. "Look who's coming."

Newton nodded to them as he arrived, and then for a moment he watched the vicar speaking to Alicia and her family. Avery had only spoken to him once since they closed the dimensional doorway, and that was briefly over the phone to let him know they could open the museum again. His dark hair was swept back, slightly ruffled in the breeze, and his eyes had dark shadows under them. He turned to Avery. "Thank you for closing the doorway. You should have called me."

"We had no idea if we could do it, and it would've been too dangerous for you to be there. Besides, you couldn't have helped."

"Even so, I'd rather know before than after—should anything like that happen again."

El jumped in, "Let's hope it doesn't. I don't want to have to deal with demons again for a while."

"Nor me," Briar said. "It's taken all week for my leg to heal."

Newton looked concerned. "Why? What happened?"

"Demons have a particularly nasty rope fire." Briar pulled her long black skirt up to reveal a dark red line that spiralled around her ankle and calf.

His face softened for a moment, and then he looked impatient. "You could all have been killed."

"So could you. You haven't got magic to protect you," Avery pointed out. "And you made it pretty clear you hate magic, and what we do. Probably best to leave you out of it."

She found Newton so confusing. He looked concerned, but also disapproving. She kept playing over in her mind what he'd said about his place in the town. He was unfathomable.

He watched her closely, his attention unnerving. "Have you decided to share with me about what's really going on?"

"No, have you?" Avery shot back.

"I'm not concealing anything," he said with searing impatience. He stood over her, his height dwarfing her, and she was forced to look up to meet his eyes.

"Neither are we," she said smoothly.

"So why did you steal from the museum?"

She hesitated for a second. "I haven't stolen anything."

He grimaced. "Really? Because there's a pen and ink drawing of Helena missing, and a book from the display."

"Maybe someone broke in after us." She kept her face straight.

He looked as if he was about to say something else when Alex, Reuben, and the others exited the mausoleum.

"Looks like we're done here," Briar said, glancing nervously between them.

"We are far from done," Newton said, and he stepped forward to join Alicia.

Alex glanced her way and nodded towards Newton, a frown on his face. She shrugged. Alex glared at Newton, and Avery sighed inwardly. More conflict.

She turned and started walking back to the church, the wind stronger now, and her long, red hair whipped around her face. She pushed it back, trying to restrain it, and mulled over the map she had found under the witch light, feeling only slightly guilty over stealing it. It was hers, really, and who knows how long it had lain there, waiting to be found. After studying it for days, she was sure that it was a map. The lines not only seemed to suggest a map, but also appeared to show the grounds of a house or a building of some sort. But she couldn't work out the key that would reveal where to start. A thought struck her suddenly. What if the grimoire was in a vault or a church crypt? It was possible. There were plenty of old churches in the town. She looked at Old Haven Church. It could even be in there.

Maybe it showed where Helena was buried? Unfortunately, that was a real mystery. Being burned at the stake meant burial in non-consecrated ground.

Avery entered the church, the high roof arching above her, and was glad to be out of the wind. It was empty now, and the smell of lilies was overpowering. She sighed and closed her eyes, pondering what to do next, but her reverie was disturbed by the doors of the church opening with a shout. "Avery, we need to go."

It was over. Time to go to the wake.

***

Alex's pub, The Wayward Son, had been closed for the afternoon, open only to mourners. However, seeing as a large amount of people from the town were at the service, the pub looked as full as usual.

Reuben had opened a large bar tab, and the wake was in full swing by the time they arrived. Food was also served, and extra staff had been drafted in to take around trays of sandwiches and canapés.

Avery grabbed a large glass of red wine from the bar and mingled with the guests, managing to find Sally and Dan and some of her other friends who she felt she'd been neglecting lately. Sally hadn't said much about Gil's death, but Avery knew she suspected something other than the official story. She finally worked her way to Reuben's side. He had taken

18

off his jacket and loosened his tie, and he had a very healthy measure of whiskey in hand. He glanced down at her, a wan smile on his face.

"I've been wanting to talk to you all day. How are you?" Avery asked, worried.

"I'm okay." He shrugged, his eyes meeting hers briefly before he glanced around the pub. "It's been a difficult few days."

"Of course. Lovely to see how many people are here, though."

"Yeah." He lowered his voice, turning away from the room slightly. "We need to meet again, I suppose. To discuss, you know…"

"When you're ready."

Reuben nodded and sighed heavily. "I've been left the house, not Alicia. That was a shock."

"Really?" Avery was surprised for a moment that he was bringing it up, and then she shook her head. "You know what—it should be left to you. It's your family home. You live there, too." Which was true. The house was huge, and he lived in a suite of rooms on one of the floors.

"I feel weird about it."

"Don't. Gil's no fool. I presume he left Alicia a good amount of money?"

He nodded. "She's not very happy. It made me think about what we were talking about the other day."

Avery recalled their conversation in the cave on Gull Island, the questions she asked about Alicia, while trying not to voice her doubts about her. Her heart started racing. "Why? Has something happened?"

"She's been weird. More than just mad at not being left the house."

Avery looked around while he was talking and saw Alicia across the room, white wine in hand, glaring at her through the crowd of people. It was as if she could hear their conversation. Avery smiled nervously and turned back to Reuben.

"I wasn't sure you'd want to be involved anymore."

"None of us has a choice," he said enigmatically. "We'll all need to meet. Just give me a few more days."

***

Alex found Avery in the back room of the pub where she'd gone to get some quiet. There was something about this room. It had a feeling of peace and space. She sat at a table on her own, gazing out the window. A fine rain had started to fall, and it blew almost sideways across the courtyard. She was debating at what time it would be polite to leave, when Alex pulled out a chair and sat opposite her.

"The table where we had our first date," he said, grinning, referring to where they'd had dinner only a short time ago.

It felt like a lifetime had passed since then. The thought was immediately followed by the memory of their night together only last week, and she tried to pull herself together. If Avery was honest, she thought about it often, not that she would tell him that.

"You're so funny."

"I know."

She decided to move on. "Have you spelled this room? It's always quiet in here."

"Maybe a little. I like to think some patrons deserve a little peace and quiet. It discourages the rowdy bunch."

Avery nodded. "I like it."

Alex leaned forward, and she could feel his body heat across the small table. "I've been thinking about the Courtney Library. We need to go tomorrow."

That was the last thing Avery had been thinking about, and she looked at him in shock. "Tomorrow?"

"Yes. We've lost a whole week. I don't want anyone else to die, Avery." He looked at her, serious suddenly. "This shit's got real. Gil's dead, there's demons and doorways to other dimensions. It's like White Haven has turned into the Hell mouth. This could just be the start. I don't like being on the back foot."

She closed her eyes and sighed for a second. "You're right. And I need help, anyway." She wondered at what point in the past week she had started trusting and relying on Alex Bonneville. *Life was really weird right now.*

"Why?" His attention was fixed solely on her. It was unnerving, like being caught in a giant floodlight.

"Helena's map. I'm stuck. I have no idea where to look."

"I'm sure we'll work it out. I'll pick you up after my shift here—that okay?"'

"Do we even know where to look?" Avery was flooded with worry, feeling unprepared.

"Trust me. And leave Newton out of this. He seems to be sniffing around a lot."

"He's a detective! That's what they do. And I'm not about to tell him I'm breaking in somewhere. *Again.*" She looked at him in disbelief.

He grunted. "Whatever."

"Have you thought any more about Alicia?"

"Not really. I've been too busy here, but it does seem to have gone quiet all of a sudden."

Avery had another thought. "I hear one of the pallbearers is a distant cousin of Gil's. Does he know magic, or about anything to do with their family history?"

Alex rolled his eyes. "I carried a coffin with him—I'm not his best mate!"

Now Avery rolled her eyes. "It was just a thought! I'll ask Reuben. Or better still, I'll ask El. Women are much better at that kind of thing."

Alex smirked. "What, gossip?"

"*Talking*. In fact, I'll do it myself." She gave him a triumphant smile.

"All right then, Miss Marple." He glanced up. "Now's your chance, he's right there."

Avery turned to see an older man with light brown hair streaked with grey in the doorway between the two rooms. He looked lost as he entered the back room, looking around a little sadly. Avery ached to see him looking so alone and she glared at Alex, an unspoken urge for an introduction.

"All right. I'll pick you up at eleven o'clock tomorrow night. Be ready." Alex rose to his feet and called out, "Lindon. There's someone I'd like you to meet."

Avery stood as Lindon approached their table, glancing between the two of them. Alex introduced them and then excused himself, leaving them alone.

"Have a seat," Avery said, smiling as she sat down and sipped her wine. "I just wanted to say how sorry I am. Gil was a really amazing man."

Lindon nodded, gazing into his own drink for a moment before looking up. Avery was struck by how similar his eyes were to Gil's. "Thank you. I haven't seen him in years, not since his wedding. I really didn't think I'd be at his funeral, too."

Avery wanted to ask him about magic, but was unsure how to go about it. "You don't live in White Haven, then?"

"No. Our side of the family decided many years ago that White Haven wasn't for us."

"Why's that?"

He looked at her quizzically. "I think you know."

She swallowed. "Maybe I do."

"My family has always thought our special skills complicated life, and I've kept away from it."

"I don't know how you do that. To me, it's as natural as breathing."

"It's like a lifelong diet—you get used to it."

Avery decided she might as well cut to the chase. "Do you know anything about your old great-uncle Addison?"

"Please don't tell me you think he had something to do with this."

Avery blinked and sat back, perplexed. That wasn't the answer she'd expected. She thought he'd look at her blankly. "Do you know him? Or know of him, and the fact that he disappeared with his family?"

"Don't you mean he was banished?"

"How can you know that when Gil didn't have a clue?"

Lindon gazed out of the window at the swirling wind and rain as it splattered across the pane. It was getting worse, gearing up into a full-on storm. He thought for a few moments and then turned to face her again, weariness as well as grief etched across his features. "He's one of the reasons we left, Avery. Black magic. He sacrificed his family for knowledge. They didn't disappear. He killed them."

Avery almost dropped her drink in shock. "How do you know *that*?"

"My great-grandmother, Felicity, was the youngest sister of Addison—we're not first cousins, just in case you wondered. There was an incident one night, screams, a trail of blood, an altar found in the woods behind the house. The details were not known to my great-grandmother, but steps were taken, and Addison was banished. He was so arrogant, he thought he could get away with it. He was wrong. Magic was a dirty word for years. That story has been told through the generations of our family as a reminder of why not to do magic at all. We don't forget."

"But that's not what magic is!" Avery cried, desperate to defend what she loved. "That was an abomination."

"Is it? Gil's dead."

"There has always been black magic, but there's always been good, too." She sensed she was losing him. "Do you know where Addison went?"

"No, I don't ever want to know." He looked at his watch. "Anyway, I'm going. I have a long drive back."

"You're not staying here tonight?"

"No, I won't stay in White Haven." He stood, easing his chair back. "It was good to meet you, Avery. I'm sorry if I sounded bleak, I know you mean well. Stay safe."

Avery watched him go, and her tears welled up. White Haven was her home, a magical place in many ways, but now, half of her wished she was leaving with him.

3

The next night, Alex arrived at eleven promptly, the engine of his Alfa Romeo Spider Boat Tail idling under her front window.

Avery slipped into his passenger seat dressed all in black—combat trousers, a t-shirt, leather jacket, and boots. "I'm not sure I'm ready for this."

He grinned, his teeth gleaming in the dim light. His hair was knotted up on the top of his head, and stubble grazed his cheeks. "You look ready," he said, easing the car down the street and heading out of the town.

"It's an illusion. I've spent most of the evening sleeping, and then panicking about being arrested. Weren't we going to scope this place out in the light first?"

"No time. We'll be fine, you worry too much."

He concentrated on the road, driving fast but confidently, and Avery leaned back in the seat, glancing between him and the view outside. The lanes of White Haven quickly turned into main roads as Alex headed for the A390 into Truro. At this hour the road was quiet and they made good time.

Sitting this close to Alex was increasingly unnerving. Avery was acutely aware of his build and height and his musky, masculine scent, and found her gaze lingering over his strong forearms and hands as they gripped the wheel. She flushed remembering the feeling of his hands on her body, and she turned away in an attempt to subdue her desire.

He broke the silence that had fallen between them. "So, how are you? The last week's been pretty rough."

"I'm okay, just getting through the day, and trying not to be paranoid about being stalked by Faversham. What about you?"

"I'm trying not to think about killing Faversham, because at the moment, that's all I want to do." He glanced across at her. "Don't you?"

"Yes, but we're not ready yet. I'm not sure I ever will be." Fear swept through her. "You don't mean that, anyway. We're not killers. We'll find another way."

"If he touches you, I *will* kill him."

Avery could barely believe her ears and for a second she struggled to think of something to say. She looked at him as he gazed fiercely ahead, and she decided to make light of it. "Well, I'll make sure he doesn't."

"I mean it."

Avery softened and smiled. "Thank you." She half wondered if she should say something about the other night, and the air in the car seemed to thicken with meaning, but she didn't want to spoil whatever it was that seemed to be there between them. She laughed to break the tension. "I hope he doesn't hurt you, either—I don't think I'm suited to a killing spree. I'm worried enough about raiding a library!"

"You're powerful, more than you know. Look what you did the other night. You were *flying* the night Gil was killed! You actually flew across that room." He glanced at her again, his eyes dark and intense. "Don't tell me you haven't been thinking about that."

"Actually, I haven't." She meant it, too. Gil's death had eclipsed everything. "It all happened in such a rush with this

26

outpouring of fury, and then Gil died, and well..."She shrugged. "I sort of forgot."

"Can you remember what caused it?"

Avery hesitated for a second as she thought back to that moment when she emerged from the passageway behind Reuben. "Pure, blind anger, and the need to stop Faversham and that rock beast from attacking you and El. I literally pulled out everything I could, really focused my power. I needed to act fast, and I knew it." She shuffled in her seat. "What about you and El? You were both channelling some strong power."

"It's ironic, isn't it? Faversham's clearly scared of us finding the books and using them, and yet the fact that he's attacking us is making us draw on reserves of power we never even knew we had."

"He accused us of wasting our power. He's probably right."

"Not anymore, we're not."

"Have you had any more visions?"

"Every night."

Avery looked at him in shock. "Really? What do they show you?"

"Versions of the same thing—black eyes, fires, heat, death. I thought they'd go after Gil died, but they haven't. Are you still reading the cards?"

"Every day. They change, of course, but the threat's still there. There's more than just Faversham, isn't there?"

"I think so," he said sadly.

For a while they made idle chat, until they entered the outskirts of Truro. By now it was after midnight and the roads were mostly empty. Alex cruised through the town, crossed the Truro River, and headed for the Royal Cornwall Museum. It was in the centre of town, and the surrounding

27

streets still had a few people exiting pubs and clubs. Alex stuck to the back streets towards The Leats and turned up a side street to park on a residential road.

"I presume they have a back door?" Avery said, her heart now beating uncomfortably fast.

"Of course. Time to use a little magic."

They had already agreed on the spell they would use, and with a short incantation they were both shrouded in shadows, the spell also ensuring that if anyone saw them, their gaze would slide away.

Avery followed Alex as his tall figure slipped through the streets to the back of the building where an inconspicuous door sat in the wall.

The museum was huge, stretching from River Street where the main entrance was, to The Leats at the back. It was constructed in the 19th century out of large blocks of grey stone, and was solid and imposing.

"Where's the library?" Avery asked, glancing down the street. It was deserted.

"You can only access it from in the museum," Alex whispered.

A security camera was mounted above them. While Alex worked on the lock, Avery used magic to manipulate the angle slightly up and across their heads, pointing away from the door. With a *click*, the door opened, and they slipped inside.

They were in a narrow passage that led into the centre of the building. Immediately to their left was a panel on the wall that housed the security system controls, and the lights blinked, starting to flash red. Alex held his hand over them and within seconds they turned green again. The pair stood still for a few moments, letting their eyes adjust to the dark, but the building was silent. Another security camera sat above them on the wall, and with a whisper Avery disabled it, the red light blinking off.

Alex conjured a witch light and led the way quickly down the passage. They passed offices and storerooms until they reached large wooden double doors, and pushing through them found themselves in the grand central hall. Avery gasped in pleasure. It rose to a high ceiling, the height of the building, and the centre of the hall was filled with glass displays of various objects. Avery took a quick look at the closest one and found that it displayed pots and ceramics that had been found in archaeological digs in Cornwall. In the centre of the room was an old carriage with huge, red wheels.

At the rear of the hall was a sweeping set of stairs that led up to the first floor. Above them, running around the room at the level of the first floor was a mezzanine, edged with a white balustrade, behind which were more display cabinets.

"This place is bigger than I thought," Avery whispered to Alex.

"This is all on their website. The front entrance is through there," he said, pointing to the far side. "I'll grab a guide."

For a few minutes Avery stood alone, hearing Alex's footsteps fading away, and she listened nervously for anything else, but he was quickly back, and he led the way up the stairs and through the galleries on the first floor. Avery paused for a few seconds when they passed the De Pass Gallery, the displays of ancient Egyptian artefacts catching her eye. Alex was quickly at her side, grabbing her hand. "I'll bring you back in the daytime if you want to sightsee," he said impatiently.

They kept going until they reached the far end of the first floor, and within minutes were in front of the double doors of the Courtney Library, its name in brass on the wall above.

The door was locked, but again they enchanted the lock open, and passed through to find a plush-carpeted section with a small reception area, and a few computer terminals behind a desk. The library stretched away ahead of them, the shelves high and densely packed with books. The smell of age-old paper was thick in the air, and Avery breathed deeply, enjoying its comforting and familiar scent.

Alex shut the door behind them and locked it again. "We need to find the archives. You head that way, and I'll try this one," he said, pointing to the right for Avery.

She nodded and passed down the stacks, seeing small rooms leading off the main one with different collections housed within. At the end of the main room was a smaller than usual black door, and she opened it to find a narrow set of stairs leading upward.

She turned and called in a low voice, "Alex!"

He appeared out of the darkness, his skin pale under the strange, luminous white of the witch light. "Found it?"

"Maybe. Did you find anything?"

"Books, books, and more books."

Avery nodded and led the way up the steep and narrow stairs. The decoration was minimal here, and the carpet was thin and worn. They reached a small landing, and after turning saw a warren of rooms with low ceilings stretching ahead of them. These must have been the old servants' quarters or attics—she wasn't sure if it had ever been a private house.

"Bollocks," Alex said. "This is a maze."

Avery's heart sank. "Do you think this is it? Because we're going to waste a lot of time if not."

Alex pointed to a sign on the wall that read, Archives. You must be accompanied by a librarian at all times.

"Great, let's make this quick."

Fortunately, the rooms were clearly signposted, their contents described in decades, subjects, or centuries.

They passed the first few, quickly dismissing them, and then came to a room on their right, labelled *Sixteenth Century Manuscripts*. Metal shelving filled with box files ran down the centre of the space.

They exchanged a quick glance of relief and headed inside, moving to either side of the central stack to search more efficiently. Every now and again Avery pulled a box out to scan its contents, and although she found lots of intriguing papers and treatises on agriculture and the local area, there was nothing about the witch trials. She stood back, frustrated, and looked up and around. A wave of tiredness and despair swept over her. *What was she doing?* She was a respectable witch. She didn't break into buildings and raid other people's property.

"I can hear you huffing from here," Alex called softly from the other side.

"Sorry. I'm having a crisis of faith."

"Don't. I'm not feeling great about this, either. But I think I've found something."

Avery found Alex on his knees rummaging through a box, its contents strewn around him. Avery dropped down next to him, searching through loose sheets of paper and a few bound books.

Alex pointed to another box above them. "I think that one's worth looking at, too."

Avery pulled it free and placed it on the floor, sifting through its contents, both of them working together, side by side. A small bound book sat in the file, and as Avery touched it, she knew. "This is it."

"It is?" Alex said, looking over. "You haven't even opened it!"

"I can tell." She opened the book excitedly, and inside, inscribed in ornate and flowery writing, was the title: *The Trials of the White Haven Witches.*

She looked at Alex in shock, her heart pounding once more. She gently turned the first few pages, and there, in the long list of the accused, she saw the name, Helena Marchmont. The emotion of the moment overcame her, and a few tears sprang to her eyes. She quickly tried to blink them back before Alex saw them. She was such a sentimental fool. But Alex had also fallen silent, and she looked around, wondering why he hadn't commented.

He was holding a very old leather book with the sign of earth on it, an upside-down triangle with a line through the bottom third—another grimoire. He raised his eyes to hers.

"You've got to be kidding me," Avery said, barely able to breathe.

"It's Briar's," he said, his eyes wide.

"Shit. We have to get out of here, and we need to take everything with us. How can *that* be here?"

"Is this a trap?"

"It can't possibly be. If Faversham knew it was here, he'd have taken it by now."

Alex opened the first few pages and swore again. "Look at the pages, Ave!"

She leaned over and saw faint white runes marked on some of the pages, only made visible by the witch light floating above them.

"Have you ever looked at your grimoire under witch light?" Avery asked.

"No. Bollocks! I feel like an idiot. Messages have been hidden under our noses the entire time!"

Alex pulled his backpack out and placed the grimoire carefully inside, then bundled some of the other papers into a cardboard file he'd bought just in case.

"Is there anything about the Favershams in those papers?" Avery asked.

He shook his head, "I'm not sure. Let's take everything."

Avery took another quick look at the book containing the trial transcripts, and saw it contained testimonies from the town members. A quick glance through the file showed a few other articles relevant to the witch trials. She hated doing this, but she copied Alex, loading everything into her own backpack.

A sudden *bang* from below made them fall silent.

"Was that a door?"

"Quickly, put the boxes back," Alex said, setting his own box back on the shelf, now empty.

They heard footsteps downstairs, and two voices calling to each other.

"Did we leave anything open down there?" Avery asked, desperately trying to remember their actions.

Alex shook his head. "No. I locked everything behind us. I doubt they'll even come up here. Maybe they've clocked that the cameras are off."

Despite the fact that her heart was now racing wildly, Avery checked the boxes on either side of the ones they'd already looked at. There was no way they'd be coming back; they had to get everything now. She was glad she checked. There were pages of interviews from witnesses—or at least that's what it looked like at first glance. She stuffed the papers in with the others, trying to be as gentle as possible while working quickly. She pushed the last box in place and ran to

Alex's side as he extinguished the witch light, and they stood still, listening together. Heavy footsteps clumped up the stairs, and they heard the door open.

Alex pulled her quickly behind the door, trying not to stumble in the dark, and wedged her in the corner so that she was blocked by his body. Avery knew that if they made a noise, their shadow spell wouldn't stand up to blazing lights.

The main light went on in the narrow hallway, and Avery pressed back against the wall, reassured to feel Alex in front of her. The floorboards creaked as the security officer paced down the hall, stopping every now and again. He must be alone. As he passed their room the flashlight flooded in, sweeping across the open space a couple of times, and then he passed on, and Avery slowly exhaled. They waited for endless minutes as he progressed slowly up and back down the hall, and then the light went off and the door shut.

Avery sagged against Alex. That was too close.

"Do we wait for them to go?" Avery asked.

"They could be here hours," he reasoned. "Let's go now."

They headed back along the corridor, creeping silently through the door and down the narrow staircase until they came to the main library. It was empty and silent, and they risked a pale witch light to guide them across to the main door where they extinguished it again and listened for noise from the galleries beyond.

With a *click* they eased the door open and stepped onto the wooden floor of the museum. It was dark; in the far distance, a flashlight swept around the corridors and two voices carried across the air.

They crept from gallery to gallery, ducking into the entrance of each one, progressing slowly onwards. The men moved down into the main hall, and then disappeared into the other galleries on the ground floor. The lighting in the display cabinets was on, and Alex and Avery glanced nervously at each other and then ran down the stairs. As they set foot in the main hall, they heard another voice approaching from the corridor that led to the rear. Avery froze for a second, and then pulled Alex to the old fashioned carriage that sat in the middle of the floor. Within seconds they were lying flat on its floor, the door shut behind them.

The carriage was small, and while she was able to lie flat between the seats with relative comfort, Alex was squashed in, pressing on top of her.

"Ouch!" Avery whispered, as Alex's weight pinned her down, his knee on her leg.

"Sorry, princess," he hissed, his mouth to her ear.

For endless seconds they heard the security guard walk around, and then they heard him speak. "Hey boss, there's no one here. We've checked upstairs and down. The boys are just finishing the back rooms now." There was silence, and then a grunt. "No. No sign of damage. No forced entry. I reckon the cameras just failed." Another moment of silence, and then, "Yeah, we're out soon."

Avery heard his footsteps fade as he headed to the other rooms.

Alex lifted his head and peered through the window. "He's gone. Let's go. Now!"

He pushed the door open, untangling himself as he pulled Avery out behind him, and then closing the door again softly, they headed down the passage leading to the back door.

Outside, a large security van was on the road, but it was empty. They ran out and onto the street, racing down towards the side street, where they slowed to a stroll as they approached Alex's car.

Avery's heart pounded in her chest, and she expected to hear a shout at any moment. Sweat was beading on her brow and she welcomed the cool night air. She hadn't even realised how hot she was feeling.

With a soft *chirp*, Alex switched off his car alarm and they jumped in. They didn't stop to congratulate themselves until they were on the outskirts of town, both of them glancing over their shoulders nervously.

Avery slumped back in her seat as they hit the A390 and sped up. "That was close."

"But successful. You coming back to mine?"

Avery felt her breath catch, and she looked at him, wide-eyed.

"Surely you want to check the grimoires under witch light?" he said with a grin.

She laughed. "Yes, I do! But I'll need a very strong coffee. Or alcohol. Or maybe both."

4

The witch light floated over the two grimoires, revealing silvery shapes magically marked onto the old paper of the spell books.

"Runes and writing," Alex murmured, gently turning the pages of his own book, as Avery looked through Briar's.

"There are marks on some pages, but not all," Avery noted.

Briar's book was as old as the others, and it contained a mixture of spells, observations on moon cycles, and experiments with herbs and gems. However, the witches who had owned this grimoire had a greater tradition of commenting on the success of the spells, or suggestions for improvements, so that it read as much as a diary as a spell book. The witch light revealed additional notes, some written in English, while some pages were marked with either a single rune or a series of runes.

Avery peered across at Alex's book. "It looks similar to this one in the way the runes are used."

Alex nodded. "There are some marking protection, others denoting months, or what I think are times to best use a particular spell. They seem to provide a hidden level of enhancement for the spells, which is weird. Why would they add a hidden message to an already very private book?"

"Added protection from prying eyes?"

Avery flicked to the unused pages in the back, the grimoire hidden before they could ever be used. Several were indeed blank, but right at the very end the witch light revealed another spell. "Look at this, Alex. This spell has been hidden completely!" She stared at the page, puzzled. "This says: Part Three, The Grounding. Where are the other parts?"

Alex quickly turned to the back pages of his own and swore. "I have Part Five, The Summoning."

They looked at each other as realisation dawned.

"One spell spread across all five grimoires?" Avery wondered, looking back at Briar's book. "I don't know what it's for. Can you tell from yours?"

He shook his head. "No. It's a just a very long spell—no ingredients. It relates to the spirit, like most of the spells in my book, but I don't understand the specifics—yet."

"There are a few ingredients in this one, and then a long chant. It's quite repetitive." Avery's thoughts raced, as she ran through the various possibilities. The spells in Briar's book were themed with the earth element, but not exclusively. "One big spell broken into five parts, each focusing on one of the elements, hidden in the back of each grimoire. The other grimoires must contain the other parts."

"One big spell," Alex repeated. "I have a bad feeling about this. There are a few reasons to split a spell."

"To make all five witches participate?"

"Yes. And to ensure everyone agreed. Or because it was too powerful for one individual alone."

"What type of spell would you want agreement on? A binding spell, or a spell to release something powerful?"

Alex sighed and looked at his watch. "I'm shattered, I can't think straight. It's nearly four in the morning.

"Is it? Wow, no wonder I'm so tired. I think adrenalin is the only thing keeping me going." Avery ran her hands through her hair, trying to release the clips that held it in a loose bun. She looked up to find Alex watching her, his eyes following her hands and her hair, and then her lips.

"Here, let me." Alex said, stepping closer and reaching for her hair clips. He tipped her head so that it rested on his chest, his hands warm on hers as he found the clips and untangled them. He put his hands in her hair, shaking it free, and it tumbled down her back. "You have the most gorgeous hair," he murmured.

Alex's warm, musky scent enveloped Avery, and she inhaled deeply, her hands resting on his chest as she pressed against him. His hands moved from her hair to caress her back, her shoulders, and then her neck, and they were so warm and strong that a sigh escaped her. He bent his head, and she felt his lips upon her neck. A shiver ran through her. This was heaven. His lips moved around her neck, kissing her gently, and then rose slowly to her cheek. As if spellbound, Avery tipped her head back and his lips blazed a trail to hers. She sank into his kiss effortlessly, like slipping into water.

Desire uncoiled within her, a slow stirring in her belly that spread deliciously around her body, her brain incapable of making a rational decision. She wrapped her arms around him, snaking under his t-shirt as he pulled her closer. His hands slid up and down her arms, leaving her tingling and breathless, and then moved to her waist. He lifted her up onto the table and she wrapped her legs around him while their kiss deepened. As her emotions ran wild, a wind once again rose around them, tugging at their hair and caressing her skin, and Alex responded, the candles around them flaring into life. Avery couldn't explain why, but the intensity of their kiss was wilder than before as an urgent lust rose

39

between them. Alex pulled back for a second, his lips grazing hers, his eyes dark with desire as he stared at her. For a moment, it seemed as if time stopped as they both hesitated, and then he picked her up and carried her through to his bedroom.

***

Avery awoke once again tangled in Alex's sheets, his body sprawled next to her. She could get used to this, she thought, as she turned over onto her back, trying not to disturb him.

Daylight filtered through the wooden blinds, casting a pale, barred light across the room. Rain was falling heavily outside. She could hear it pounding on the roof, and it cocooned the flat, drowning out all other noise. Alex felt warm, his arm heavy, and she gently traced the dark shapes of the tattoo that ran across his shoulders and down his arms.

Part of her was annoyed that once again she'd failed to show any willpower at all, but the other half didn't care. She wasn't sure if this was leading anywhere, but it felt good while it lasted. Avery had never felt like this about anyone. It was partly because they were both witches. He knew her, but they also had a connection, a spark that she couldn't explain. No doubt he'd break her heart, but she was resigned to it. As long as she was expecting it, maybe it wouldn't feel so bad when the inevitable happened. She inwardly rolled her eyes. She was such a fool. And then she remembered what he'd said last night about Faversham. I would kill him he if touched you. She probably shouldn't read too much into that.

Alex stirred and mumbled into her shoulder. "It feels late."

"It *is* late. It's after twelve."

"Thank the gods I'm not working." He opened his eyes, squinting at her. "I need coffee."

She smiled. "I can get it."

"No, let me. My machine's temperamental. Want one?"

She felt cheeky. "Yes, please. Do I get brunch, too?"

He grinned at her. "Sure. But only if you stick around all day."

She twisted to look at him. "Why do I have to stick around?"

"Well, a—why wouldn't you want to? And b—we have work to do. All that stuff we found last night." He nuzzled her neck again. "I promise I'll make it worth your time."

She thought she might just stop breathing. "You don't have to bribe me with sex."

"It's not bribery. It's a pleasure. Isn't it?" he asked, his eyes questioning as he held her gaze.

"You know it is," Avery said, almost whispering it.

"Good," he agreed softly, before kissing her again. And then he slid out of bed and walked naked across the room and out to the kitchen. She couldn't help but watch him, admiring his long muscled limbs, his flat stomach, and his toned abs. *He was so hot.* She flopped back on the pillow and looked up at the ceiling. *I'm screwed*, she thought, *literally and figuratively.*

Alex cooked an amazing brunch of hash browns, eggs, and bacon, and she gazed at him with new appreciation. He moved competently around the kitchen, and grinned when he saw her watching.

"I didn't know you could cook," she said.

"Must you always underestimate me?" he chided. But she could tell he was pleased.

As soon as they'd eaten, they spread all of the papers they found in the archive on the sofa, the table, and the floor. Avery called Briar with the good news about her grimoire, and the others had agreed to come over later that afternoon.

41

"I wish I'd thought to bring the picture of Helena's hanging and the ledger," Avery said, making herself comfortable on the sofa. She curled up in the corner, the book containing the trial transcripts and the extra papers about Helena's trial next to her.

"What we find here may make it easier to understand the map, anyway," Alex reasoned. He sat on the rug, the other papers next to him, and the grimoires on the table.

For a while, they worked quietly together. The book containing the trial notes was difficult to read, the language awkward, and the writing faded in places. The first trials were of some old women who had been accused of turning milk sour by a local farmer, as well as ruining crops. Another had been accused of causing a stillbirth. Avery sighed. This was common during the witch trials, and both men and women were the accusers. It was impossible to say now, but more than likely these poor women had had nothing to do with what they were accused of. From the small amount of information available, these women were old widows, living on little money, and struggling to get by.

Initially, the numbers accused were low, and then a fury seemed to ignite the town, and more women's names appeared, along with a few men. Avery's blood chilled. It must have been terrifying. The trials all resulted in a test of witchcraft by drowning. Those who survived were hanged, but most drowned anyway. At this stage there was no mention of burning witches at the stake.

There were a few witness statements at the beginning, defending some of the poor accused, but as time went on, these grew less and less, as those who tried to defend them soon found themselves on the list of accused. And then Helena's name appeared and Avery hesitated for a second, almost scared to read further.

She must have sighed, because Alex called over, "You okay?"

She looked up at him. He had a witch light hovering above his shoulder, illuminating his grimoire and Briar's next to it. "I've just come across Helena's name. This is so horrible. I don't want to read it, but I have to."

"Do you want me to?"

"No. It's fine. I'm being stupid. But I can't help but imagine what if that happened now. What if someone saw a demon, and we were accused in some way?"

"No one would believe it. They'd be locked up in the nearest psychiatric ward. Besides, we could get around that with a spell."

"Could we? Helena couldn't."

"You don't know what happened yet," he reminded her.

"You're right," she said. "I need to focus."

Avery went back to the transcript and had her first shock. Helena was accused as Helena Marchmont, widow of Edward Marchmont, and mother of Ava, aged eight, and Louisa, aged five. *Helena was a widow.* This left her vulnerable. Edward had been a merchant, but Helena had no occupation, and that would fit. She wouldn't need to work as the wife of a merchant. They had money and status—if he'd left her some, which was likely. It was odd, but the address listed was different from the one she had from Anne. Maybe this was a later address. The cottage she'd found on the edge of the town wouldn't have befitted a merchant. Maybe this was Helena's family's home. With any luck, Avery would be able to find the house she shared with her husband. She sighed again and kept reading.

The first charge against Helena was listed on the 9th of October 1589, and they went back several years. A man called Timothy Williams had accused her of killing his wife when she lost her child and then died in childbirth. He said she had done it deliberately, as they were rivals in business. Others had defended her, saying she was a respectable woman who helped her community. Avery recognised the Ashworths' (Briar's family), the Bonnevilles', and the Jacksons' names. They were listed as merchants, too. Again, that made sense, particularly the Jacksons. And then the transcript mentioned another accuser. *The Favershams.* Thaddeus Faversham stated that his wife had almost died in childbirth, but had survived by the grace of God. Their child, however, had died after being cursed by Helena Marchmont, who had attended the birth. He then went on to list failed shipments that had been run aground because of storms. He accused Helena Marchmont of making those storms. Thaddeus cited evidence that Helena's mother had been known as wise woman and witch, and that clearly she had inherited her skills. Joseph Marchmont, Helena's brother-in-law, had defended her, but then it seemed the two girls were threatened. Avery could imagine his fear. Helena stood accused, but he had to protect his nieces.

Then Thaddeus accused the Jacksons, the Bonnevilles, and the Ashworths, too, but none of these seemed to hold weight—at least they weren't formally charged. Maybe they were just too well known and respected. And then someone called Elijah James accused Helena.

Avery felt a rush of anger. Williams, James, and Faversham must have been working together, and maybe had scared others into accusing Helena of witchcraft, too. She did not and would not believe that Helena would be capable of harming others.

Helena had been found guilty. It was impossible to know the details between these lines of accusations—the transcript was dry and devoid of emotion—but whatever the defendants had said hadn't worked, and Avery wasn't sure if they could risk any more for her.

It was interesting that so many of them were merchants in some way or another. Maybe the Favershams had threatened their families, businesses, and livelihoods. One way or another, the accusers had won. A date was set, October 31st, and Helena was burnt at the stake.

And it seemed that Helena was the last name accused, as if her burning had ended the madness. Maybe the town had been appalled at what had happened.

Avery sighed again and looked up to find Alex watching her. "This is horrible."

"Go on, tell me."

She related the story, and as she talked, the events made a little more sense, but she still felt there was something unsaid, something significant. *Why would a witch threaten another in such a public way, just for business?*

Alex tried to reassure her. "Everybody went a bit mad at these witch trials—they whipped people into a frenzy, for a while at least, and then it settled down again. It doesn't excuse their behaviours, though. They were different times, Avery. But, it's interesting that the Favershams led the attack. It could be business motivations, or it could be a cover for something to do with magic. What happened to her children?"

"I don't know. I presume their Uncle Joseph looked after them, or maybe Helena's mother. There's no further mention of her here, so maybe she was in hiding, or had died. I'll have to check my family tree."

He nodded at the pile of old yellow papers next to her. "What's in those?"

"I don't know. I haven't got to them yet." She looked around at the darkened room. The rain was now lashing the windows, the wind surging against the building. She could hear the crash of the surf on the beach. She couldn't see the harbour, but she knew from long experience that the boats would be bobbing furiously, the pavements would be empty, and the pubs would be full. However, it was nice to be curled up on Alex's sofa, even if her reading material was grim. She smiled at him. "How are you getting on?"

"Okay. There are commonalities in the rune markings on certain spells, but I'd like to check the other books first. I still don't know what the spells in the back are about." He shivered. "It's getting cold." He looked at the kindling in the fireplace, and suddenly flames flashed along them and onto the logs laid across them, and then the candles around his flat sparked to life, along with a couple of corner lamps.

Avery groaned. "I am not looking forward to leaving here later. I'm going to get soaked."

"You can stay here," he said.

She shook her head, "I can't. The cats need feeding, and I have work in the morning."

"I'll run you back, it won't take long."

"Thanks," she said, already wishing she didn't have to go, even though she wouldn't be leaving for hours yet.

She turned back to the other loose papers and with a shock, realised they were letters. They were addressed to the magistrate, and they were from Thaddeus Faversham. An even bigger shock was the name of the magistrate. She cried out and looked up at Alex, momentarily too stunned to speak.

"What?" he asked, his eyes narrowing in concern.

"I've found Newton's connection. The magistrate—or Justice of the Peace—was named Peter Newton."

Alex looked stunned. "I presume it would be too big a coincidence not to be related at all to our DI Newton."

46

Avery's mind raced as she filtered through a few possibilities. "He condemned Helena to death, and many others. Newton said, 'I know my place in the town.' Is he here to protect us, or condemn us?"

"Or protect the town *from* us?" Alex reasoned.

Avery felt vulnerable and looked around the room, as if someone would burst in on them and drag them away.

Alex tried to reassure her. "Avery, it's okay. *We'll* be okay. I won't let anything happen to us—I promise. And neither will you. You're too strong." He nodded at the papers in her lap. "Read the letters, hopefully they'll fill in the gaps."

She nodded and turned back to the letters; there were about five in total. Again, the writing and the language were difficult to decipher, but she persevered, determined to get to the bottom of whatever happened.

After about half an hour, a glass of red wine appeared in front of her. Avery looked up to find Alex grinning. "I thought you'd need fortification. You're miles away. Good news or bad?"

She smiled and took the glass from him, taking a sip before speaking. "Thanks. Well, the news is good and bad. The JP was not running the witch trials, the Witchfinder was. The JP was involved because of his position in the town. He had to be, but it seems he was an unwilling participant. The first letters are from Faversham to Newton, basically complaining about Helena based on the charges he bought against her. It seems they were a polite necessity, basically warning him to support him. There's a letter from Newton telling him to, more or less, consider his actions carefully, and Faversham replied basically telling him to butt out. Then the Witchfinder sent a letter warning Newton that to try to defend Helena would be dangerous, perhaps suggesting his support of witchcraft."

Alex sat next to Avery on the sofa, a bottle of beer in hand, and he took a letter from her, scanning it as she spoke. "So, basically, Peter Newton was damned whatever he did. If he tried to support her, his life and family were endangered."

Avery leaned back against the sofa, looking up to the ceiling. "The bastards. Helena never had a chance."

"But what did she *do*, Avery? And if Faversham was a witch, which he must have been, why didn't he seek revenge using magic? Why use the Witchfinder?"

Avery turned to look at him. "You're right. That's a great question."

He looked smug. "I know. I'm awesome."

She rolled her eyes. "And so modest."

"Anything else in these?" He gestured at the papers.

"Not really, other than really wordy ways of threatening people. Odiousness must run in the Faversham family. The Witchfinder sounds vile, too."

"That doesn't surprise me. But the good thing is, Newton's ancestor wasn't that bad after all."

"He was spineless."

"He was threatened," Alex reminded her. "Maybe that's what our Newton meant by *his place*. Maybe his ancestor was so angry and helpless that since then the entire family line has vowed to protect White Haven and the witches in it."

"He's got a funny way of going about it," Avery mumbled.

"It's a hell of a legacy. Especially if you don't have much choice."

5

It wasn't long before El and Briar arrived, bringing pizza. Avery felt a little self-conscious at already being there with Alex. She felt sure they would know what they'd been up to, and while it really didn't matter, she felt nervous anyway. But neither of them said anything, although Briar did look at Avery with raised eyebrows and the briefest of smirks. Avery attempted her wide-eyed look of innocence, and knew she'd failed immediately when Briar smirked even more. El, however, headed straight to the kitchen with boxes of pizzas, barely glancing at them.

Avery decided to change the unspoken subject. "Where's Reuben?"

El sighed. "He'll be here when he's ready."

The others exchanged worried looks, and Briar shook her head as a warning.

"He's grieving, El. We need to give him time," Alex said.

"I know. I just wish he wasn't angry with me."

"I'm sure he's mad at everyone right now."

"No. Just me." Her tone didn't invite further questions.

This time Briar changed the subject, and grinned broadly. "So, where's my grimoire?"

"Voila, madam," Alex said, pointing towards the coffee table.

Briar gave a barely suppressed squeal that was distinctly un-Briarlike and ran to look at it. "I can't believe it! It's just beautiful."

"I need to show you both something," Alex said. "El, we need your grimoire, too."

El pulled her grimoire from her pack and handed it over. Unfortunately, she didn't look anywhere near as excited as Briar.

"Come over here," Alex said, drawing her to the coffee table, where he placed her book down next to the others. "I just hope this works with yours, too."

El looked mystified as Alex put out the lamps and conjured a witch light above the books. As he'd hoped, El's book also showed hidden runes and writing.

All of a sudden, El's grim mood disappeared and she sat next to Briar. "What? How? It's just like the book we found in the witch museum. I didn't even think! I'm so annoyed with myself..." she trailed off, turning the pages of her book.

"We need to check the back pages, if that's okay?"

El looked puzzled. "Sure, but why?"

Alex didn't answer as he turned to the end, and there, revealed by the witch light was another spell: *Part Two, To Seal with Fire.*

El gasped. "What's that?"

Alex sighed. "In the back of each grimoire is part of a spell. We think they make up one large spell, but we're not sure what it does. Again, yours has no ingredients, like mine, just a spell—a chant. You have part two, I have part five. Briar, you have part three."

El and Briar looked from Alex to Avery and back again.

"I'll sort food," Avery said to Alex. "You explain."

She headed to the kitchen, putting out olives, cheese, and crackers, plus the pizza, hoping that Reuben wouldn't leave them waiting long—if he came at all. She listened as she worked, smiling as the others looked through their grimoires, comparing runes. She was surprised by how comfortable she felt with them all, although really, why shouldn't she? She had spent the last few years keeping her distance from them, and now she wondered why she had. They knew her, understood her, in ways no one else could, even her oldest friends.

And Alex. She paused for a second, watching him. His long hair was loose, falling about his shoulders, his face animated as he talked through the runes he'd found. Whatever preconceptions she'd initially had about him were being slowly eroded away. He was thoughtful, funny, and sexy, and he felt genuine. As if he'd heard her thoughts, he looked up, holding her gaze for a second, before returning to his explanations. *Oh my goddess*, she thought, *be still my beating heart.*

"These runes," he continued, "give protection. It must be a way of categorising the spells. But these," he said, pointing to a few different pages, "add words or extra instructions to the spell. This suggests working with another witch."

"But why wouldn't you put that in the body of the spell?" El asked. "It doesn't make sense."

"This one here," he continued, pointing to another spell in his own grimoire, "suggests an extra ingredient—vervain—and adds a warning: *to lock the heart forever.*"

Briar nodded. "Vervain works better if secrecy is attached to its use. Maybe it was thought to hide it within the spell would add potency."

"Interesting," El murmured. "Like a spell within a spell."

But instead of answering, Alex went still, his face clouding over, his eyes gazing into the unknown.

"Alex!" El shouted. "What's happening?"

Avery dropped the knife she was holding with a clatter. "Don't touch him!" she shouted. "He must be having a vision."

El and Briar both sat back, giving Alex some space. Briar said, "I've never seen this happen before."

"No, nor me," Avery said, watching from the kitchen. "But he said he's getting them regularly."

For a few seconds they watched Alex as he remained immovable. His eyes flickered rapidly and his breathing became shallow, but otherwise he was as still as a statue. Just when Avery was beginning to wonder how long was normal for a vision to last, Alex blinked and looked around, bewildered.

"Are you all right?" Briar asked, narrowing her eyes with concern.

"I am, but Reuben's in trouble."

"*What?*" El leapt to her feet, almost overturning a candle. "Where is he?"

"On the outskirts of White Haven," Alex said, stumbling to his feet. "I'll drive."

"No. I'll drive," El said with white-faced fury. "Keys," she commanded, and her keys flew across the room and into her hand.

Without hesitation she raced down the stairs, the others following. Avery helped Alex, who still seemed dazed. He paused briefly to seal the room.

"Maybe you should stay here," she suggested to him as she waited.

"Not a chance. I'll be fine in a minute."

Within minutes they were outside, piling into El's battered old Land Rover, and El spun the tyres as she floored the accelerator, racing through the pouring rain.

"Where?" she shouted.

"Old Haven Church," Alex said.

Briar sat next to El, flexing her fingers, muttering softly to herself as she summoned her powers, and Avery joined her, trying to calm her shattered thoughts. *Please let Reuben be okay*, she thought.

"Who was there, Alex?" El called over her shoulder.

"Faversham, and a woman I didn't recognise."

"A woman? Not Alicia, then?" Avery asked.

"Why the hell would it be Alicia?" Briar asked, spinning round to look at them.

"Just a thought I had. I'll explain later," Avery hedged, bracing herself against the seat in front, as El rounded a corner way too quickly.

Briar glared at her. "Don't kill us, El!"

El ignored her, concentrating on the road. Avery turned back to Alex. "Who?"

"I don't know. I couldn't see features, just the sense of a woman. Dark hair maybe?"

"Fuck it!" El yelled, as she got stuck behind a car. As soon as she could, she veered around it, turning onto the lane that led to Old Haven Church.

The rain continued to pour down, and wind whipped the branches of the overhanging trees against the car. The lane was narrow, and if an oncoming car headed their way it would be a disaster. El didn't care. She floored it, and Avery used her magic to help keep the rain away from the car, trying to sense if anything was in front of them.

She turned to Alex. "Did you sense anything else? I mean, was Reuben in the main church?"

He closed his eyes and frowned. "I sensed anger and desperation more than anything. There was a damp smell. I think it was maybe the mausoleum? I don't know." He looked up at her, anguished.

Avery thought of Reuben mourning his brother in silence and then being attacked, and her chest tightened with renewed worry.

Within minutes El was hurtling into the car park at the church. Reuben's car, an old VW Variant, was parked there on its own. They piled out of the door and ran towards the church, drenched before they'd even reached the wide sheltered porch in front of the locked door. It was deserted. El set off again, the others following, running down the path towards the mausoleum, and that's when Avery saw dark smoke spiralling into the air.

The mausoleum door hung at an angle, and a woman with long, dark hair was directing blasts of energy like lightning towards the building. Avery could see a large crack in the wall from here, and the tree that sheltered the mausoleum smouldered. No one else was in sight, and it was clear that she couldn't see the approaching group. El sent a blistering rope of fire at the woman, which snaked around her legs and pulled her to the ground. She turned, her face vicious, even though she was sprawled on the floor. Briar stopped and the rest ran on, but within a few feet, a massive crack erupted down the middle of the path, almost causing Avery to fall. The crack widened under the fallen woman, and although she was struggling to her feet, it knocked her off balance, and she fell into an ever widening, dark hole.

The woman stretched out her arm and flung a blast of energy towards them, causing Avery and El to dive out of the way on either side of the path, but Alex stood firm, holding his hands up and out. Avery wasn't sure quite what he did, but the wave of energy stopped abruptly as the woman screamed and fell to her knees, engulfed now in mud as the earth started to swallow her whole. They were close now, within a few feet, and able to see the woman struggling for control.

Avery squinted through the rain, slicking her hair back from her face, and saw a large, broken branch to the side of the mausoleum, brought down by the wind. She used the wild energy of the wind that raced around her as if it recognised her, and pulling the branch up into a vortex of air, smashed it on to the woman's head. She fell, unconscious, to the ground.

El raced onwards to the mausoleum, and Avery followed, skidding to a halt in the entrance. Reuben was unconscious on the floor, blood streaming from a wound on his temple. El rushed to his side, dropping to her knees and feeling his pulse, while Avery stood panting behind, looking around for any sign of Faversham. But the room was empty, other than for the coffins of Reuben's family; Gil's rested on a shelf, looking far too new.

A wave of sadness and anger, and the weight of centuries pressed down on Avery, and she took a deep breath, trying to steady her breathing. She turned back to the grounds and saw Alex and Briar standing over the woman. They were all completely soaked now, the woman drenched and covered in mud where the earth had pulled her in. Avery shuddered. She had almost been buried alive, and Avery wasn't sure how eager she would have been to save her. She turned back to El. "Is he okay?"

El nodded, looking relieved. "He's unconscious, but alive."

Alex and Briar arrived at the mausoleum, and Alex nodded at the woman. "What the hell are we going to do with her?"

"I want to interrogate her!" El said, looking furious. Avery was shocked; she had never seen El like this.

"I'm all for defending myself, El, but I'm not attacking her now that she's down," Alex said, frowning at her.

"And where's her car?" Briar asked. "How did she get here?"

"The same swirling cloak and dagger way Faversham does, I suppose. I'd love to know how they do that!" Avery said.

Over the sound of the wind and falling rain, Avery thought she heard something else. A car engine. "Someone's here."

Alex ran to El's side. "Let's get Reuben up and we'll drag him to the car. That woman can stay here. I don't care if she gets pneumonia."

But as Avery looked back to the church, she saw two things—the tall, dark-haired form of Newton rounding the corner of the church, and then the unmistakable, blurred shape of Faversham appearing next to the fallen woman.

Faversham hesitated for a second, looking at Avery and back at Newton, who now started sprinting towards them. Faversham knelt down and grabbed the woman's hand, and then with a whirl of wind, he disappeared, taking her with him.

Within seconds, Newton arrived at the mausoleum and sheltered under the porch. He shook water off his jacket, and slicked it out of his hair and off his face. He glanced back at the broken earth, at Reuben's unconscious body, and then at the cracked wall and the smouldering tree, before looking at their bedraggled appearances.

"I think we need to talk."

6

"I think now would be a good time for you to tell me exactly what's going on!" Newton yelled.

He stood in the middle of Alex's living room, soaking wet, trying to towel himself dry with an enormous bath towel. He scrubbed at his clothes and rubbed his hair with fury, until it was standing up on end. He was wearing casual clothes, jeans and a t-shirt, with an old university hoodie, so that despite his anger, he seemed far more approachable now than he had been before. His drenching had removed some of his command.

Alex stood opposite him, also soaking wet, and also trying to dry himself while shouting. "I think it's pretty clear what's going on. Our friend Reuben was attacked and almost killed. Would you like me to file a report?"

"Only if you think you could explain what the hell happened. I'm not sure magic really qualifies for a good statement."

"Well, magic pretty much sums it up," Alex said snarkily.

"Start from the beginning. And tell me everything."

"First, tell me how you knew we were there." Alex demanded, his eyes narrowed with suspicion.

"One of my colleagues had spotted you hurtling up the lane and called it in. I've asked for everyone to watch your cars for suspicious activities."

"Really! You're spying on us?" Alex asked, incredulous.

"For your own good," Newton shot back.

"We're not bloody children!"

"No. You're just unleashing magic onto an unsuspecting community," Newton said dryly.

"Actually, no, we're not! The only people we're unleashing our magic on are other witches who are intent on doing us harm and stealing our grimoires! Witches we didn't know even existed."

Newton stared icily at Alex. "But innocent people have been hurt in the process."

"Not by us."

"Tell me *everything*," Newton repeated.

Alex glanced questioningly at Avery, and she nodded.

Alex sighed and started to explain.

Avery looked from one man to the other, mildly amused, but also slightly amazed at their antagonism towards each other. They were like chalk and cheese, and she decided not to get involved.

She sat in front of the blazing fire, wrapped in a blanket after towelling her hair dry. Reuben was lying on Alex's bed, where Briar was using her healing spells, trying to bring him back to consciousness. El was with her. She presumed they'd call if they needed any help. Avery reckoned Alex must have dished out every towel and blanket he owned.

It was dark outside now, the fury of the storm continuing unabated. They had returned to Alex's flat a little under half an hour ago. They had all helped carry Reuben to the car park, and then split into groups. Briar and Avery brought back Reuben's car, with him on the back seat, while Alex returned with El. Newton had followed behind. Avery had driven, and stopped briefly at Briar's place for her to pick up some herbs and gemstones that she needed for healing. She lived in a tiny cottage tucked on one of the town's back streets, and Avery had waited in the car, and then swung by her own flat to feed her cats. She wasn't sure what time she'd end up getting home later. She was relieved to find that her wards remained sealed.

A huge rumble of thunder cracked overhead and Avery jumped, jolting her out of her reverie.

Newton scowled again, his arms crossed in front of his chest. "You have no idea who the woman is?"

"No," Alex said patiently. "I have never seen her before in my life, but she was trying to bring the mausoleum down on Reuben's head. She meant to kill him. We need a plan."

Alex was right. Faversham had killed Gil, and now they were all at risk; they had to fight back. Before she could think coherently she needed food. The smell of warmed pizza filled the flat, and Avery dragged herself from the fire and over to the kitchen. She pulled out plates and cutting boards and placed the three pizzas out, grabbing a slice for herself.

"Hey, guys, you should eat." She pushed plates towards them, and then carried some through to Briar and El.

The bedroom was only lit by candlelight, and the sweet smell of incense drifted across the room. Briar sat cross-legged on the bed next to Reuben. She had placed healing stones on certain points of his body, a poultice on his head wound, and she held his hand as she quietly whispered a spell.

El looked up as Avery entered, her expression grim.

Avery placed a plate with a couple of slices of hot pizza into El's hand.

El shook her head. "I can't eat."

"I don't care. Try. Force yourself."

El rolled her eyes, and took a bite, chewing unenthusiastically.

"How's he doing?"

"All right. Briar's amazing. She's been sitting like that for the past 20 minutes. His breathing is stable, and his colour's good."

Avery smiled, relief washing through her. "Do we know why he was in the mausoleum?

"To spend time with Gil? I don't know, we haven't talked in days." El's pale blue eyes filled with tears again.

"It'll be okay. Just give him time."

El nodded and turned away.

Avery headed back to the living room and did a double-take. Newton and Alex were leaning on the counter, a slice of pizza in one hand, a bottle of beer in the other. They still looked antagonistic, but clearly hunger had exhausted them.

"Any idea why Reuben was at the church?" Avery asked. "The weather's foul. It just seems odd to me."

"I've no idea. I'm too tired to do this right now," Alex said.

Avery sighed and reached for another slice of pizza. "Me, too. But we need to hide where we are from Faversham. I feel like we have a homing beacon on us. Reuben was a sitting duck on his own. Especially in the middle of a deserted graveyard."

Newton looked at them, frowning. "So, how long has Faversham been involved?"

Avery shrugged. "Since the beginning. We think he's the one responsible for the demons."

"So, he's the one responsible for killing the woman in the car and the cleaner in the museum?'

"Maybe," Alex said. "He did kill Gil. We saw it."

"I think that was a pretty important thing to leave out of your statement," Newton said, clearly annoyed.

"He conjured a bloody great rock monster and slammed Gil against the wall. If it hadn't been for Avery, we'd probably all be dead. How would you like me to phrase *that* in a statement?"

Newton looked as if he would argue, but then he nodded and sighed.

Avery decided she'd had enough of secrets. "Newton, you need to tell us about your part in this. You know magic, you know us. We've levelled with you, now please, be honest."

"You haven't told me everything, Avery."

"We've told you a lot."

"What are the hidden grimoires?" He leaned against the counter, watching her.

It didn't seem worth lying about anything else to him. It was strange, but despite the little they knew of him, she trusted him. "They're our old family grimoires, hidden from the Witchfinder General back in the 16th century. From what we can piece together, Helena—my ancestor—was betrayed, or set up by her accusers—the Favershams—and burnt at the stake. The other families tried to argue for her, but it didn't work, and after she died, they moved and the grimoires were lost, until now. We're still foggy on the details. "

Alex added, "We don't have all of the grimoires—only three. Faversham threatened us to get them. He wasn't joking."

Newton groaned and put his last bite of pizza on the counter. He looked at Avery and Alex, his grey eyes tired. "All my life I have been warned about this, warned that it may happen in my generation, but we are always warned, and then the threat passes. But now it seems it's true."

Alex looked nervous. "What's true?"

"That my real job is just starting."

Avery gaped. "What are you talking about?"

"The soul of old Octavia Faversham is bound with a demon's and lies somewhere beneath White Haven. Your ancestors put it there, and it's my job to keep it there."

Alex looked stunned. "Is that a joke?"

"No, unfortunately not." Newton looked as sane as anyone could after uttering such a bizarre sentence.

A horrible trickle of fear ran down Avery's spine. "The spell in the back of the grimoires. Is that what it is? A binding spell?"

"It could be. I have no idea where they put Octavia's soul, or how they did it. I just know it was performed by all the witches to contain Octavia and her pet demon, and as a threat to the rest of the Favershams to back off."

"And you didn't think to tell us?" Alex asked, furious again. "You've known, all this time!"

Newton looked at the floor, and then back at Alex. "I didn't *know*. This information is passed down, generation to generation. How do I know what's relevant or not? I never really believed it, if I'm honest." He appealed to both of them. "I mean seriously, demons?"

He had a point, Avery had to admit. She could scarcely believe it herself, and she was a witch.

"And," Newton continued, "these *activities* have only happened a few times before. Approximately once every century."

Avery sighed. "Addison Jackson."

Newton narrowed his eyes. "Yes. How did you know?"

"Anne's research—Gil's cousin. I've been trying to build a picture as to what happened to Addison. But Lindon said he committed black magic—killed his family for the grimoires."

"No. That was a lie that was fed to his family and descendants. He fled, with his wife and children into hiding to protect them. I believe he did use black magic—blood magic—to conceal them. But he didn't kill them. I'm hoping he had a happy, peaceful life."

"Oh, great," Alex said. "He just left Gil's side of the family to mop up the mess."

"I didn't say he was perfect," Newton said, reaching for another slice of pizza.

Avery's head was reeling, and she was pleased to see Alex looked just as shocked. "The Favershams threatened him back then?"

"So I've been told. And the times before then, too, in other generations. There's a reason witches leave White Haven."

"Yeah, so I keep being told, too," Alex agreed. "Well, it ends here. I refuse to be chased out of my town by some thieving necromancer and his crooked family. And when we find the other grimoires, we'll be more powerful and far harder to manipulate."

"Hold on," Avery said, thinking furiously. "The grimoires have two functions. They detail powerful spells that we've never come across before, and they contain one hidden binding spell that was used to bind Octavia Faversham and her demon. We have no idea what Faversham wants, but presumably the latter. Does this mean they want to break out Octavia's soul?"

Alex looked baffled. "I guess so."

"But why? What relevance does it have? I mean, what did she do that was so bad that she was bound in the first place, and why is it so important to release her and her pet demon? They have demons coming out of their ears!"

"Didn't your demon-hunting, White Haven-saving ancestors pass that one down, Newton?" Alex asked.

"It seems not," Newton snapped. "I guess your demon-binding, soul-snatching ancestors didn't, either."

Oh great, Avery thought. *Testosterone.* "Guys, we need a plan. You said it, Alex. We're being attacked. Gil's been killed. This is not a game. We need to protect ourselves, and work out a way to attack them first. I hate being on the back foot. And, who are they? We need to know! Faversham and who?"

"Well, I guess that's where I come in," Newton said. "I have access to records you can't get to. I'll check out Faversham's family, his contacts, everyone. Then we'll know who we're up against."

***

They spent the rest of the evening waiting for Reuben to wake, and looking at the grimoires and the documents.

Newton was behaving less like a policeman and more like a friend. Avery had offered to show him what they'd found and he sat on the sofa, looking through the papers and the transcripts of the trial.

"What's your first name?" Avery asked Newton. She was sitting on the floor next to Alex, looking through the three spell books, a witch light hovering between them. "I mean, calling you Newton seems rude."

He looked up, the ghost of a smile on his face. "Mathias, or Matt, but everyone calls me Newton, so you can stick with that."

"Fair enough. What do you think of the papers?"

"Interesting. And chilling. I don't suppose you'd care to tell me where you found them?"

"Not really," Alex said, bristling for an argument again.

Newton raised his eyebrows. "Probably for the best. I've heard about my ancestors and the Witchfinder General, but

64

reading these threatening letters makes it more real. It makes my blood boil, actually."

"At least your ancestor wasn't burnt at the stake," Avery pointed out.

Newton nodded, "True."

Briar came out of the bedroom and stretched. "*Now* I need pizza. Is there some left?"

"Is Reuben okay?" Avery asked.

"He's fine. It was touch and go for a while—his head injury was huge, and his arm was badly bruised." Briar looked shattered, but still very pretty. Her long, dark hair was half tied on top of her head, the rest cascaded down her shoulders. She wore a long, dark red summer dress that set off her hair, and made her skin look even paler. Newton did a double-take, and leapt to his feet.

"Sit down, Briar, let me." He ushered her to the sofa, and then went to get her some food and a glass of wine. Briar seemed oblivious to his attentiveness, but Avery wasn't. Maybe something good would come out of this after all.

Briar sank into her usual corner and within seconds Newton had handed her a glass of wine. "Pizza will be a few more minutes," he said.

"I'm fine," she said, flustered. "Don't rush."

But Newton was already busying himself in the kitchen.

"How's El?" Alex asked.

"Panic-stricken. Things aren't good with those two. Reuben's in a bad space right now."

"Not surprising, but he'll come round, he's a good guy."

"I'm not so sure. He's blaming her for Gil becoming involved in the search for the grimoire."

Avery was stunned. "Why? That doesn't make sense. It was Reuben who pushed Gil to search for it."

"He's looking to blame anyone now. Of course he's blaming Faversham, but El got caught in it, too."

"Why not me? I'm the one who got the box in the first place."

"I think there's a bit of anger in there for all of us," Briar said sadly. "I can't say I blame him."

Newton sat next to her and handed her a plate stacked with pizza, cheeses, and olives. "There you go."

"Thank you," she said, and gave him a beaming smile. "So how are you involved in all this, Newton?"

"Long story."

"I've got time."

Newton started to explain about his family history and Alex nudged Avery, whispering in her ear. "I'm thinking of leaving El and Reuben here tonight. Can I come back to yours?"

"Of course," she stuttered, feeling a rush of pleasure that he'd asked.

"Cool," he said, and leaned a little closer, the warmth of his skin against hers making her tingle. He pointed at the hidden spell in the back of Briar's book. "Briar's book is all about healing, of course, but there are some interesting earth spells, too. This hidden spell, the one we think may be the binding spell, seems to tie the spell to a certain spot."

"Does it? How?" Avery leaned closer, pushing her hair behind her ears.

"This part here." Alex pointed to a line. "The place within the centre of the pentagram, there shall the binding be strongest, rooted to the earth, anchored by the elements, for all of time as the spell desires."

"Within the pentagram? What pentagram?"

"Well, that's the big question, isn't it?" he said, his gaze travelling down to her lips. "Do you think we can get away with leaving now?"

She flushed and grinned. "I don't think so."

"Go on. You know you want to." He smiled mischievously.

"You're a very bad influence," she whispered back, a thrill of anticipation running through her.

"I know. Fun, though." Alex looked up at Briar, interrupting her conversation with Newton. "Do you think Reuben will wake tonight?"

"I hope not. I'm hoping a long, natural sleep will help him heal. Sorry Alex, you've lost your bed for the night."

"In that case, I'm taking Avery back home, and you two can leave when you're ready. I'm going to let El sleep here, too."

Briar's eyes widened in surprise as she looked between Alex and Avery, and then a smile spread across her face. "Fair enough. I'll hang around for another hour or two, just in case there's a problem, and then I'll go home, too."

Newton looked speculatively at Alex and Avery, and then back to Briar. "I'll wait with you, Briar, and then take you home. In fact, from now on, we should all keep an eye on each other."

"Er, okay," Briar agreed, "thank you."

"That reminds me," Alex said, rising to his feet. "Me and Reuben had been thinking about a design of some runes that can hide us from Faversham. The only thing is, it needs to be a tattoo for full protection. Interested?"

Newton frowned. "For me as well?"

"You're part of the team now. You're as much at risk as the rest of us."

"I'll think on it."

"Me, too," Briar said.

"Good." Alex pulled Avery to her feet. "Give me a couple of minutes, and I'm good to go."

7

Alex and Avery were woken the next morning by a loud banging on the front door.

Avery groaned and rolled over to look at the clock. "Crap, it's barely seven! Who's that?"

"I'll go," Alex said, already rolling out of bed and pulling on his jeans and t-shirt.

Avery thought she'd better follow him, although it was unlikely Faversham would just knock at her door. She hurriedly pulled her jeans and t-shirt on, too, ran her hands through her hair, and raced downstairs after Alex.

She heard El's voice before she'd got halfway down. "You have to stop him, Alex! He'll get himself killed, and he won't listen to me!"

El was standing in the middle of Avery's living room, tears streaming down her face. Her face was red and her eyes swollen.

"What's happened?" Avery asked, fear running through her.

Alex was already reaching for his phone that was lying on the kitchen workbench.

"Reuben's gone to confront Faversham."

"He's done what?" Avery said, horrified.

El started crying again. "He woke up half an hour ago and has gone mad. He couldn't remember what had happened for a second, and then when he did he just yelled, and said he was going to kill Faversham." She gasped to get her breath, blinking back tears. "I tried to stop him, but he won't listen. He barely looks at me! We have to stop him."

"He's taken his car, I presume?"

"Yeah. He grabbed the keys and just ran out."

Avery found her own keys, "Alex, let's go."

Alex was on his phone. "It goes to voicemail."

"Keep trying, I'll drive. Try and get Newton, too."

They raced to Avery's car, and she pulled out onto the quiet streets. "I'll follow the main road to Harecombe, that would be the quickest way."

She navigated the streets, trying to keep calm, while Alex called Briar. He sat next to her in the front seat, El sitting anxiously in the back. She had fallen quiet now, looking out of the windows, desperate to see a sign of Reuben. The weather was still foul, the wind and rain battering the car.

"Hey, Briar," Alex said into the phone. "Is Newton with you?" He raised his eyebrows at Avery. "Sorry, Briar, no need to yell. Have you got his number? I need to speak to him urgently. Reuben's gone to attack Faversham." He paused and listened. "We're going after him now, on the road to Harecombe. Can you tell Newton? Great, see you later. Don't worry."

"Did you upset her—about Newton?"

Alex looked sheepish. "I think so. She said not to be so bloody presumptuous."

Avery laughed. "I needed that bit of levity right now." She looked at El in her rear view mirror. "Are you okay, El?"

Elspeth continued to look out of the window. "No. I'm worried sick."

"I'm sorry he's mad at you. It's not your fault. If it's anyone's, it's mine."

"No, it's not!" Alex said, annoyed. He turned to face Avery and El behind him. "It's Faversham's. He's the dick here, not us. These are our books. It's not our fault his ancestor, Octavia was such a bitch that she was locked up in some sort of witch's purgatory with her bloody demon."

Now El looked surprised, her attention finally off Reuben. "What the hell are you talking about?"

"Oh! You didn't hear Newton's news yesterday, did you? It's a shocker." He sighed and started to tell her.

Avery half listened, racing down the lanes that led to Harecombe. Once the road opened up, she put her foot down, going as fast as her ancient van allowed. The road hugged the coast, twisting every so often and giving flashes of the sea and coves along the way. There was no way they'd catch him. Then she had another thought. "Hey guys, where am I going in Harecombe? Where does Faversham live?"

"That's a great question," Alex said. "El?"

She looked dumbfounded. "No idea. I'm still trying to process witch purgatory."

"So I'm racing down this road to *where*?" Avery asked, increasingly frustrated.

"There!" El yelled, pointing out the window towards a car park above the beach where Reuben's car was parked.

Avery slammed the brakes on, and turned onto the road to the cove. "What's he doing there?"

"His surfboard's missing." El said, relief creeping into her voice. "Maybe he's changed his mind."

"Maybe he's realised that like us, he has no idea where he's going," Alex said.

"Maybe he's got a death wish," Avery put in. "Surely the weather's too bad to surf. How's he got his wet suit?"

"He always has one in the car," El said.

They pulled up next to his car, right at the edge of the otherwise deserted car park, and looked over to the cove below. The path down to the beach travelled through sand dunes until it hit the beach. The tide was in, smashing against the beach and the rocks either side of the cove. Avery could see Reuben on his board, trying to make his way out.

"Shit. He's really trying to surf now?" Alex was incredulous. "He'll be crushed."

"How the hell do we stop him?" Avery asked, knowing no one could answer.

El jumped out of the car and raced down the path, drenched in seconds. They heard her voice, the words lost on the wind.

"Oh, crap. What now?"

Alex sighed and looked at her. "I suppose we need to go after them."

"And do what? There must be a spell we can use." Neither was dressed for the weather, and Alex looked as rumpled as she felt. "I don't think I'm even really awake yet."

"This was not how I imagined this morning would start."

"Alex, get your mind off sex. Our friends are in crisis."

"A crisis that will not be solved by us getting soaked on the beach. We're going back to bed after this."

"Seriously. Stop it. What is wrong with you?" Avery looked at him in amazement. "Our friend is possibly trying to kill himself!"

"Nothing's wrong with me. For a start, I don't think he's trying to kill himself. I think he's trying to blow off steam, and surfing is Reuben's way of doing that. He surfs. A lot. For hours. He's very good at it. And I woke up in bed with a beautiful woman. Why wouldn't I be thinking of sex?" He grinned suggestively.

Avery was momentarily flummoxed. *Did he just call her beautiful?* "I'm not beautiful."

"Yes, you are." Alex looked away, frowning. "What's he doing?"

Avery followed his gaze, and saw Reuben had paddled out a long way and was standing up on his surfboard, facing out to sea. He seemed to be gesturing towards the waves. Slowly but surely, the waves were starting to rise. El stood on the shore, looking as if she was shouting at him.

"Is he doing that wave thing?" Avery asked, shocked.

The waves rose higher and higher, swelling beneath Reuben, who had dropped to a crouch, looking far too small and vulnerable.

"Oh, shit." Alex said abruptly, getting out of the car and running towards the beach. Avery followed, the wind and the rain shattering her peaceful mood.

Within seconds she was soaked, and she raced down the path, pushing her hair out of her eyes. She could hear Alex shouting. "El, get back, get back!"

But El was already turning and running back towards them.

The giant wave beneath Reuben started to fold and Reuben plunged with it, riding it towards the shore. Avery stopped dead on the wooden path, watching nervously. It looked terrifying.

For a few seconds he disappeared beneath the swell of the collapsing wave, and then he shot out through the end, the spray ferocious.

Alex was up ahead and he had grabbed El's hand, running back with her. The wave hit the shore where El had stood only seconds earlier and raced up the sands. Reuben maintained his balance, crouched, arms outstretched as the wave brought him to the shallows, and as the wave disappeared, he paddled to shore. The waves had crashed just below the sand dunes, and Avery ran to join El and Alex, who stood on the boardwalk just above the water line. Driftwood and seaweed lay strewn across the beach, abandoned by the receding wave.

Alex looked furious and El looked shocked. The wave was lethal, it could have killed Reuben and El. Didn't he see her?

Reuben stood on the shore, looking back at them.

"Wait here," Alex said, and ran to Reuben.

Avery pulled El towards her. "Are you all right?"

El was crying. "What's he doing?"

"He's grieving, El."

"He could have killed me."

"He probably didn't see you." Avery reasoned, trying to reassure herself as well as El.

"I never thought I'd say this, Avery, but I can't look at Reuben right now." El rubbed her eyes and then wrapped her arms around herself. "I want to go."

Avery looked beyond El to where Alex stood in front of Reuben. They were almost nose-to-nose, and Alex looked tense, his fists clenched at his side. He looked over his shoulder, gesturing towards them. Reuben looked across to them and then turned and walked away, back into the sea.

"Come on," Avery said. "Alex will catch up." She turned away and led El up to the car.

8

They dropped El at home. Avery had suggested she came to her flat, but she refused.

"I wouldn't be good company right now, and I've got jewellery to make and a grimoire to study."

Avery looked at Alex after she'd left. "Did Reuben make that wave, knowing El was there?"

Alex still looked annoyed and had been quiet on their way back—all of them had. "I don't know, though I don't think so. But he sure didn't look too worried when I pointed out he could have drowned her."

"It must have been a mistake," Avery said. "Reuben's not like that."

"No, of course not. But it doesn't mean he can't be a jerk occasionally."

"Is he still going after Faversham?"

"No. Even he knows that's dumb right now." He sighed, looking out at the harbour next to El's flat. "My mind really isn't on work right now. If there's enough staff to cover me, do you mind if I come back to yours?

Avery smiled. "Of course not, although I'm supposed to be working too. I'll ask Sally if she can manage without me today; I really want to go through that stuff again. Do you need anything from your flat?"

"I want to check that it's secure. Not quite sure how Reuben and El left it earlier."

"Sure. I'll let Briar know that Newton can stand down," she said with a grin.

The summer storm showed no sign of stopping, and after picking up some food and a few beers, they parked behind Avery's flat and raced through the rain and into her home.

The cats meowed loudly. "I better feed these guys," Avery said as they snaked around her wet ankles, demanding attention. She bent over, patting their sleek heads.

"And then I think we need a shower," Alex declared, puddles of water forming at his feet. "I might die from pneumonia."

Avery looked him up and down and grinned. His clothes clung to him, revealing every well-placed muscle. "You look pretty good wet."

"I look even better wet and naked. How big is your shower?"

"Not big enough for two," she said, laughing.

"Damn it," he moaned in mock frustration. "Shall I leave it running for you?"

"Yes, please."

He headed up the stairs, and after Avery had fed the cats, she lit a few lamps, brightening the gloom. Her bright Persian rug and colourful cushions glowed in the warm light, and she opened the window an inch, enjoying the smell of the wet earth and the sound of the rain. Alex was singing in the shower. She smiled. She could get used to this.

She unpacked the bags of food, and then headed up to the shower, stripping off her soggy jeans and t-shirt, until she was only in her underwear. Alex was heading out of the bathroom as she went in. A towel was wrapped low on his hips, revealing his tanned, toned abs and arms, and he rubbed his hair dry with another towel. She couldn't help but stare.

He lifted his head, catching her looking, and grinned as he took in her lack of clothes. "Now this is what I was thinking about when I woke up this morning," he said, reaching for her with a wicked grin.

***

After one of Alex's amazing breakfasts, they headed up to the attic, and surrounded themselves with Anne's research and the map they had found at the museum.

The rain sounded even louder in the attic, thundering on the roof and against the windows. Avery put some music on in the background, and then lit a few candles and some incense to aid concentration.

Alex picked up Avery's family tree. "It's hard to believe that Anne spent years doing this research."

"Do you think she knew it would turn out like this?" Avery sat cross-legged on the sofa, the hidden map on her lap.

"No idea. Did she know your grandmother?" Alex looked at her curiously. He was sitting on the rug, leaning against a large Moroccan leather pouffe.

"I'm not sure. I'm planning to see her this week—she lives in the nursing home in Mevagissey. I'll ask her then." Avery frowned. "I'm not sure it will be much good. Her memories have gone, she can't even remember who I am half the time."

"Alzheimer's?" Alex asked, looking concerned.

"Unfortunately."

"They say that the memories of their youth can stick around longer than those of the present. She may surprise you."

"Maybe. She would have been a contemporary of Anne and Lottie. They must have known each other."

"Did she tell you much when she was younger and well?"

Avery grimaced as she tried to remember. "I could kick myself. I never asked anything when I should have. Magic was our family secret, of course, and we knew about you and Gil, obviously. I was told we were special and that we mustn't tell anyone, but as I grew older, I didn't ask questions. It was what it was. My grandmother taught me the old ways—the herbs and their properties, the powers of stones, the tarot."

"Not your mother or father?"

"My father left when I was young. There was my mother, my sister, and me. And my gran. So yes, my mom did teach me some stuff, but she was never comfortable with it. And my sister wasn't interested at all."

"Could she use magic, though? I mean, did they have the power, or was it dormant?" Magic could skip generations, or could be suppressed or not used. Like any skill, you could lose it over time.

"A bit of both, I think. They thought it unnatural."

Alex nodded. It was a familiar story, as Gil's cousin proved. Not everyone welcomed magic into their life. "Same for me. My father used it, occasionally. He was prone to strong psychic visions, and he hated them. It all freaked my brother out completely. My uncle pretended it didn't exist, and ran the pub for normality."

Avery leaned forward, her elbow on her knee, and her chin in her hand. "Where's your dad now?"

"A long way from here. Scotland."

"Why Scotland?"

"Because it's a long way from here. He swears it dulls his visions."

"What about your mother?"

Alex fell silent for a moment. "Magic didn't run in her family. She found it fascinating, and then she got bored with the weirdness of it."

"So, who taught you?"

"My dad, haphazardly. I didn't respect it enough when I was younger. I took it for granted."

"You were cocky."

He smiled slowly, holding her gaze. "Yes, I was cocky. About lots of things."

Avery was fascinated. "So, when did you start to respect it?"

"When I was about 18 and it finally sank in that no one could do what we could do. I wanted to learn more about it, about me, who I was, and I knew I couldn't learn any more from my dad. I think his powers scared him." He looked at her speculatively. "I couldn't ask you. You kept me at arm's length."

"I did not!"

"Yes, you did. I was cocky. I get it. Your gran would offer me the occasional cup of tea. I should have taken her up on them more often."

"I didn't know that!" Avery felt a rush of guilt. If Alex was lonely and needed guidance, she never knew it. She probably needed some herself.

He carried on, undisturbed. "Gil was a bit older, more serious, and already involved in the family business. El had just arrived, Briar wasn't here then. So I went travelling."

"So I gathered. Where to?"

"India, of course, where everyone goes for spiritual guidance. And maybe weed."

She laughed. "What did you learn about magic there?"

"Not magic so much, but just who I was. I needed to get out of our quaint English seaside town. I travelled around, lived a little, partied a lot, and got dysentery. Then I went to Ireland. I loved it there. I could *feel* magic in the soil. And then I met an old guy on the West Coast of Ireland. He knew when he looked at me."

"Knew what?" Avery asked, confused.

"Knew that I knew magic."

Now Avery was really curious. "Another witch?"

Alex's eyes darkened with memory. "Yes. He must have sensed I was lost. He took me in and taught me how to use my powers, how to spirit walk, how not be scared of my visions, but to trust them."

Avery slowly sat up, seeing Alex in a new light. She'd noticed how different he was over the last few weeks, but talking about this with him was like uncovering another layer.

"That's amazing, Alex. How wonderful for you! Who was he?"

"His name was Johnny, and he lived in an old ramshackle cottage on the edge of the sea on the Ring of Kerry. He never told me his full name, but he knew magic, Avery, really knew it."

"Did he have a family, children?"

"If he did, he never spoke of them. I had the feeling they had gone away a long time before." Alex looked sad as he recalled his memories.

"How long did you stay there?"

"A couple of years, and then I knew it was time to come back. Part of me didn't want to leave—he's old, and I was worried about him. But he knew it was time, too. Said I had to leave, that something called from White Haven that could not be refused. And he was right, so I came."

"So when you arrived here a few months ago, you'd come straight from him?"

Alex nodded.

"Do you hear from him?"

"Occasionally. He only has a land line, and half the time he won't answer it, but I call him anyway." He smiled. "So, that's my story. I haven't told anyone about Johnny before— I'd appreciate it if you keep it quiet."

Avery felt a rush of pleasure that he'd told her such a secret. "Of course, scouts honour," she said seriously. "Was he psychic? Did he know what we'd find?"

"Maybe. He never said what it was." Alex paused for a moment. "What do you know of other witches, outside of White Haven?"

Avery considered his question for a second; she had never been asked that before. "I know nothing of other witches, although I accept the probability."

"There are more of us out there than you realise, Avery. Johnny told me about others."

"How many?"

"I don't know. But like us, they live together in small communities. That's why I reconnected with you and the others when I returned. I wanted all of us to work together. And if there are other witches, I want to know them too."

"But what if they're like the Favershams?"

"What if they're like us?" he challenged, watching her reaction. "If our problems with Faversham get really big, we may need help."

9

Avery's grandmother sat in an armchair in front of a big picture window looking out over the sea. She was petite, white-haired, with bright blue eyes that weren't quite focussed on the view outside.

The residential home sat on a high cliff looking out over the bay beyond. The summer storm had gone, and the sun sparkled off the white-tipped waves. The garden below was filled with roses and summer flowers, and the occasional resident and visitor pottered along the paths.

Avery sat in the chair opposite her grandmother and placed two cups of tea between them.

"Hi Gran, it's me, Avery. How are you?"

The old lady looked at her with flicker of recognition that was quickly gone. She smiled. "I'm all right, my dear. Do I know you?"

"I'm Avery," she repeated, her heart sinking. "Your granddaughter. Diana's child."

Her gran nodded. "I had a daughter called Diana. She was headstrong, that one. Always getting into trouble." She gazed out to sea again. "I miss her."

Avery closed her eyes briefly. This was always so hard. She chatted for a while about what she'd been doing, and asked her gran if she'd been out. Her gran responded, chattering for a while aimlessly, and seemed happy enough.

Avery decided now was a good time to broach what she'd really come to ask. Sometimes calling her by her name worked. "Clea. Do you remember Lottie Jackson?"

She turned to Avery, frowning. "Lottie was a nice girl. We used to meet for tea and talk about magic sometimes."

Avery looked around in alarm, hoping no one was close enough to hear. Fortunately, they were the only ones in the sunroom.

"And what about her uncle, Addison? Do you remember him?"

Her eyes clouded over for a second. "He was always a strange one. We were told to keep away from him."

Avery sat forward. "Why was that, Clea? Can you remember?"

She shuddered and once again turned her gaze to sea. "He disappeared young. Those Faversham boys, causing trouble again."

Avery nearly fell off her seat in shock. "Did you say Faversham?"

Her gran turned in alarm. "Shush! We never say their name. It's bad luck. Almost brought down the whole Council on us once."

Avery's head was whirling. "What Council?"

Her gran frowned. "Do I know you?"

Avery bit back her impatience, and patted her gran's hand. "I'm Avery, your granddaughter."

She smiled. "Of course you are. You look so pretty. Just like Diana."

"You mentioned the Council?"

She looked impatient. "Their water rates are so high! It's scandalous."

Avery blinked. This was useless. What was she thinking? She leaned back in the chair and closed her eyes. She was so tired. After talking to Alex the other afternoon, and reading Anne's papers, she felt she was on the cusp of knowing something, but it was fragile, just beyond her grasp.

She opened her eyes and watched her gran stir sugar into her tea, her hands shaking lightly. She was so old now, so infirm. She wondered if she retained any magic, or if the Alzheimer's had suppressed it. And then she realised her gran's spoon was stirring all on its own. She gasped and pulled it out of the cup. She hoped this didn't happen often.

Some core part of her was still there, buried deep. Avery had to try again.

"Why was the Council upset about the Favershams?"

"Oh, they weren't upset with them, they were upset with us."

"With us? Why?"

"Those hidden books caused a lot of trouble. Everybody wanted them." Her gran looked at her earnestly. "We promised not to look for them, and were forbidden to mention them again." She put her finger in front of her lips, her eyes wide. "Silly people. You can't hide magic."

Avery felt a shock run through her. What the hell was going on? "Clea. It's very important. Who are the Council?"

"They're not really a Council," Gran said crossly. "It's all pretend. Some people just like to give themselves airs. We pretended to listen for a while, and then Lottie had a plan. They didn't know that." She broke off, looking perplexed. "I wonder what Anne did with it all? Is there any cake, dear?"

"I'll get you cake in a minute. Who are they, Gran?"

"Nasty people," she said. "There's a reason witches left White Haven."

***

Avery arrived at her shop, her head whirling. Despite her best attempts, and lots of bribery with cake, she got no more sense out of her gran.

It was unnerving. The more she found out, the less she felt she knew. Who were 'they?' Why did they call themselves a Council? And most importantly, where were they now?

Sally was standing at the counter, and she looked up as the bell rang on the back of the door as Avery entered. Her blonde hair was taken back into a high ponytail, her reading glasses were perched on the end of her nose, and a pile of new books was stacked on the counter in front of her. "You okay?"

Avery nodded, burying her confusion. "I'm fine. Just stuff on my mind."

She took a deep breath, inhaling the smell of incense and books. Just being here calmed her down. And of course her spell on the place, designed to ease people's moods and help them concentrate. Jazz was playing in the background, Sally's favourite, and a few shoppers perused the aisles.

Sally grinned. "Alex popped in."

"Great. Is he okay?" Avery asked, non-committal. She plonked her bag on the counter and reached for the sweets jar they kept stocked for customers.

"You tell me. You seem to be seeing a lot of him. He had a spring in his step and a twinkle in his eye." She narrowed her eyes. "So do you."

Avery considered her answer, looking at Sally with a raised eyebrow. She didn't want to reveal quite how much she'd fallen for him. "We've reached an understanding. He makes me laugh."

Sally smirked. "I bet he does more than that!"

"Sally!" Avery said, fake scandalised.

"Lucky cow. So, come on, give me the details. Don't think I didn't see his car here the other morning."

"Reuben was at his flat, actually."

Sally snorted. "Yeah, right. So he slept on the sofa?"

"I'm not saying any more."

"I'm teasing," she said, her voice softening. "And pleased for you. Now, get behind here, you slacker, I have stock to check."

"Bring me a coffee?" Avery asked, as she settled in behind the counter.

She nodded and disappeared into the back of the shop.

For the next half an hour, Avery dealt with customers, in between texting El and Briar to see how they were. They all planned to meet up the following evening to swap news, just as Reuben stepped into the shop.

His glanced around the aisles, and then headed to the counter. He looked pale, despite his deep tan. He was wearing a surf t-shirt, shorts, flip-flops and sunglasses. His blond hair was tussled and salt-crusted. He slipped his sunglasses onto his head, and Avery tried not to show her surprise. He looked exhausted.

"How you doin', Reuben?" she asked him, concerned.

He shook his head. "Not great. I came to apologise about the other day. I'm having trouble processing things."

"Not surprisingly," Avery said, her heart heavy. "I'm so sorry, for all of this."

"I didn't mean to put you in danger."

"It was El who was in danger, not me."

He dropped his head. "I know. I've rung her, but she's not answering. She won't answer the door for me, either."

"She'll come around. She was pretty pissed, though." She hesitated a second and then added, "You're both doing a good job of pissing each other off, actually."

Reuben nodded and fell silent, glancing around the room again to check that no one was within earshot. "I want justice for Gil. It seems Faversham is just getting away with murder."

"He won't. We just need to work out what we're going to do. Have you heard about Newton?"

"Yeah, Alex filled me in."

"We're meeting him tomorrow. He's finding out everything he can. We have to do this the witch way, not the legal way."

He nodded, but he still looked down. "Sounds good."

"We'll do this, Reuben," she said softly.

He swallowed and looked her in the eye, his gaze direct and unflinching. "We'd better. Anyway, there's something else I need to talk to you about—two things, actually. Are you free this evening?"

"Sure, why?"

"You need to get a tattoo. I've arranged it all with Nils." Nils was Reuben's friend who owned the local tattoo shop, Viking Ink. "He's staying open late tonight to get us all tattooed."

They'd been talking about this for days. "So you've finished the design, then?"

"Yep, me and Alex. We all get the same tattoo, and it should protect us from prying eyes. And that will help for my second request."

Avery had a flutter of worry. "Which is?"

"I need help. I think I know where my book is."

Avery's glanced around paranoid. "Really?"

"Come to Old Haven Church later. I've texted Alex. I want him there, too."

"Er, sure. What time?"

"Just before midnight."

"Midnight?" Avery wasn't sure she wanted to be wandering about some creepy old church at night.

"It has to be. Trust me." He headed for the door, and then turned back. "Don't bring El." And then he disappeared, striding past the window and down the street, leaving Avery wondering what was really going on.

10

Viking Ink tattoo parlour was located on the floor above an arcade that was packed with kids and teenagers. It was accessible by a narrow staircase, and at the top, the staircase turned and the door opened in a long, airy room.

Big picture windows showed views of the street below, and between the buildings opposite were glimpses of the sea and the harbour. The walls were covered in tattoo designs, the floor was wood, and there were a few partitioned rooms leading off from the main space.

Nils, the owner, was the Viking of his shop name. He was Swedish, and huge. Well over six feet, with enormous shoulders, chest, and well, everything really, Avery concluded. His biceps and forearms were well muscled, and he had a long, red beard and a completely shaven head. And of course he was covered with tattoos. Avery could see the complex designs spiralling down his arms and peaking above his V-neck shirt. He was wearing jeans, so she had no idea if his legs were tattooed, but the likelihood was high.

She'd seen him around White Haven—you couldn't miss him—but she didn't really know him. He was vaguely terrifying, purely because of his size and aggressive look. He had the palest blue eyes, almost icy, and that really didn't help. Avery could imagine him let loose with a massive axe, invading his way across Europe hundreds of years ago.

He looked up as she entered and almost grunted. "We're closed." His words held a trace of his Swedish accent.

She stopped suddenly in the doorway. She was the first to arrive. "Reuben told me to come. I'm his friend, Avery."

"Ah! Avery, come in!" He grinned, showing the whitest teeth, and his scary demeanour vanished. He strode across the room and engulfed her hand in his large one. It was without doubt the strongest handshake she had ever experienced, and she tried not to wince. "So good to meet you. Lucky you! You're the first, come and have a seat."

"Oh, great," she said, trying to sound enthusiastic.

"You are in some club, yes? You're all having matching tattoos."

Avery laughed nervously. "I'm not sure you'd call it a club, but yes, matching tattoos."

He led her to the counter and pulled a sheet of paper towards him. "It's a cool design. Rune work and a pentacle. Very Viking—I approve."

"May I see it?" Avery asked.

"Yeah, sure," he said, his deep voice booming around the room as he handed her the design. "Where we putting this bad boy?"

The design was a complex layering of runes around the outer circle of a pentagram and a protective sigil in the centre, all in black ink. "How big will it be?"

"About the size of your hand."

"Oh." That was bigger than she'd thought, which sounded more painful. "Can I have it on my hip?"

"Sure, right or left?"

"Right, I guess." Avery was so unprepared for this.

A woman came out of a back room as they were talking and nodded at Avery. Avery was momentarily silenced. She was a beautiful, young Japanese woman. Her long, dark hair was tied back, and a section on either side of her head was shaved. She was covered in gorgeous, inky black tattoos, flowers trailing all the way up her arms and at the base of her neck.

Nils started collecting his equipment together. "This is Chihiro," he said. "She's helping me tonight."

Chihiro nodded, but didn't speak. She sat behind the counter and picked up a magazine.

"When are your friends arriving?" Nils asked.

"Soon, I guess."

"Great, I'll start on you. Next one's yours, Chi," he instructed.

He led Avery to a small, partitioned room. "Lie on the table, drop your skirt, and wriggle under the sheet on the bed." He gestured to the long table like a masseuse's bench down the centre of the room. Bright lights were above it, casting a good, even light.

As Avery was getting ready, she heard the door open and Briar shouted out, "Hello?"

"I'm in here, Briar," Avery called, glad of the company.

Briar appeared at the door and looked at Avery with a grin. "Wow, so we're really doing this?"

Nils smiled at her. "Chihiro's doing you. Will be about an hour or so."

"An hour?" Avery exclaimed, her voice muffled as she dropped her head into the space in the table.

Avery was vaguely aware of Briar disappearing, then she heard the *whir* of the needle start, gritted her teeth, and closed her eyes.

When she finally got off the table, her skin burning, Alex and El were also in the main room, debating who was going next. Alex grinned at her. "How's it feel?"

"Painful."

He laughed, "It'll soon go. You bandaged up?"

"Sure she is," Nils said, coming out of the room after her. "Follow the instructions. It looks good. Who's next?" he asked.

"Ladies first," Alex said, nodding to El.

El had already got a couple of tattoos on her upper arm, and appeared to know Nils. "Hey Nils, it's been a while."

"Ah, beautiful Elspeth, come in honey," he said with a wink.

Avery could hear the needle whirring in another room, and presumed Briar was still in there. She sat next to Alex. "That really hurt."

"It won't last long. Sorry I missed the start, the pub was busy." He leaned in and kissed her, his hand cradling the back of her neck as he pulled her close. "I missed you."

"It's only been a day," she said, secretly pleased.

"That's enough. Did Reuben ask you about tonight?"

"Yeah. I'm intrigued, and a little worried."

"I'll feel happier once these tattoos are on. We need to enchant them to activate their power," he explained.

She nodded. "Are we doing that together?"

"May as well."

Avery looked up as the door opened again and Newton walked in. She'd almost forgotten he'd be getting tattooed, too.

Newton looked around the room, taking everything in, and then sat on a worn leather chair next to Alex. He was once again dressed in his work suit and a dark grey shirt. "It's been a while since I've been in one of these places."

"You've got a tattoo?" Avery asked, surprised.

"Yep. A big wolf on my right shoulder."

Alex nodded. "Sounds cool. Where you gonna put this one?"

"Top of my left arm. You?"

Alex looked down at his arms. "No room there. It'll go on my left shoulder."

They were interrupted by Chihiro joining them in the main room, followed by Briar. Newton rose swiftly to his feet. "Briar, are you okay?"

She looked slightly embarrassed as well as pleased, and she held a hand to the base of her neck, securing the dressing in place. "I'm fine. I can cope with ink and my own blood."

Chihiro eyed Alex with pleasure. He stood to greet her, and she reached up and kissed him on the cheek. "Alex, it's been too long." She stood back to appraise him, and Avery felt a trickle of jealousy run up her spine. "You look good," she said, her voice low.

"You too, Chi," he said softly. "You doing my ink? You did the rest!"

"It would be my pleasure," she said, a smile playing across her lips.

I'll bet it would, Avery thought, trying not to snort with derision. She was pretty sure Chihiro had done more than give Alex his tattoos.

As if he'd read her mind, he looked at Avery. "Meet at yours at nine? We can complete everything."

"Yeah, if you know what you're doing?"

He winked. "Trust me."

***

Close to midnight, Avery stood with Alex at the entrance to the Jackson's mausoleum, waiting for Reuben to arrive.

The door was sealed shut, but a huge crack still ran across the stone work from the foundation to the roof.

"I hope the roof doesn't collapse on our heads," Avery said, looking out to the church and the cemetery.

"It's stood here for centuries, battered by the elements. I'm sure it can withstand a little magic," Alex said.

They had met at her flat a few hours earlier as arranged, and together with Briar, El, and Newton, they had recited the spell that activated their protective tattoo. Newton had looked uncomfortable throughout the whole ceremony, but hadn't complained once. His grey eyes watched Briar discretely, and he stood near to her whenever possible.

They drank a potion that Alex had brought with him, and then repeated the spell after him: By day, by night, dispel might, harbour love, harbour life. By air, by fire, by earth, by water, let us pass unseen, unheard, our spirits hidden.

As soon as they had completed the spell, Avery felt a flare of power on her tattoo, and the sensation of being branded with fire had flashed into her mind before it vanished.

As uncomfortable as it had been, she felt relieved it had been done. Hopefully they'd have no more surprise visits from Faversham. Reuben hadn't joined them; Alex said he'd already completed his spell. El merely nodded, and Avery wondered if anything would be the same between her and Reuben again.

As she was thinking of him, she saw headlights beyond the church, and heard the low growl of an engine and the crunch of gravel.

Within minutes, Reuben was at their side. "You haven't gone in, then?"

"No thanks, mate," Alex said. "It's a bit creepy in there."

"Fair enough," Reuben said. "Have you been tattooed?"

"All done," Avery said. "Nils and Chihiro are interesting characters."

"I'd trust them with my life," Reuben said. "Follow me."

He held his hand over the lock, and muttering a few words softly, they heard the lock release. Reuben turned the large handle and pushed the door open.

"What are we doing here?" Alex said, a hand on Reuben's arm, before he went in.

"I think I've found a hidden entrance. It might be where my grimoire is. After the last time, I thought I'd bring some back-up."

They followed him into the cold, damp building and closed the door behind them. Several doors led off from the main room. Stone sarcophagi were stacked high and deep, and Avery was surprised by the size of it. Her gaze involuntarily fell on Gil's coffin, before she turned to follow Reuben into a small side room.

"This is the oldest part of the mausoleum," he said. "I've been studying old plans, and something looked unusual here."

Avery was incredulous. "You have a blueprint of this place?"

"We have plans of everything. The grounds, the glasshouse, the ice house, the main house, old garden plans, even the old gatehouse. I grabbed all the prints I could find and hid them in part of the attic. But, things have been added to over the years, so I'm not sure how accurate everything is."

"So, this is what you were looking for the other day," Alex concluded, looking around with interest. He flashed his torch around the corners and high ceilings.

"Yes, before I was attacked by that bastard."

"You feeling okay now?" Avery asked.

"Yeah, thanks to you guys and Briar." He turned away, shining his torch down to where a coffin lay on a low shelf, inset into the solid stone wall, a gap of about three feet between it and the floor. "It's here somewhere."

An ornate design of curling plants and flowers had been carved into the stone around a name—*Prentice Jackson, 1388 – 1445*.

Avery gasped. "Is this the oldest grave in here?"

Reuben looked up at her from where he now knelt in front of the stonework, a grim smile on his face. "I think so."

"When was this built?"

"About the early 1400s. Before then, our family was buried in the graveyard. Prentice built this."

"Wow. Most of your ancestors in one place." She wondered where hers were buried, and realised she hadn't even thought about it before—other than about Helena.

Reuben trained his light on one flower, and turned to them, smiling. "Look."

They leaned closer. Within the centre was a simple pentagram, hidden within the design of the plant, the petals curling away from it. You would never see it if you didn't look closely. Reuben pushed it with his finger, and it receded into the stone around it with a click.

For a second, nothing happened, and then the whole stone shelf and the sarcophagus on it started to scrape back into the wall.

Avery's breath caught in her throat and goose bumps rose along her skin. This was seriously creepy. She looked back over her shoulder, but the dark shadows remained unmoving.

Alex asked, "Is that another passageway?"

"We're going to find many more before this is over," Reuben said, watching the space grow bigger and bigger before sticking into position. Stale, damp air wafted up from the dark hole. "Alex, help me push."

Alex got down on his hands and knees next to Reuben and pushed the stone further back; it scraped across the floor painfully and Avery winced. Reuben flashed his torchlight into the space. Shallow steps led downwards.

Reuben grinned, his face shadowed grotesquely. "Shall we?"

Avery's skin prickled. "Seriously?"

"You could stay here if you prefer?" he offered reasonably.

"No, thanks," Avery said, wishing she was still in her warm flat.

"It's okay, Avery. I'll follow you," Alex said. "We'll be fine."

Avery followed Reuben down the steps and grimaced as the cold, damp air hit her skin like a clammy hand. She pulled her coat tighter around herself, and sent up a witch light, in addition to her torch.

The steps were steep, but on the right, the wall opened out and they were soon on the floor of another square stone chamber beneath the mausoleum. Two long stone benches ran along either side of the room. In the centre was a crude fire pit, and at the far end was a carving in the wall—images of the Goddess and the Hunter. Beneath it was an altar, made from rough hewn stone. Brass lanterns hung overhead, spaced across the ceiling at regular intervals.

Alex snapped his fingers and each one lit with a bright orange flame.

"Is this a place of worship?" Avery asked, looking around in shock.

Reuben looked just as surprised. "Looks like it."

"What better way to hide your magical practices than down here," Alex said, pacing around the room.

"But look at the floor," Reuben said. "Devil traps and pentacles."

He was right. Carved into the stone were ornate diagrams and a huge pentagram.

Avery wandered over to the altar. A ritual knife still sat there, next to a goblet and a tarnished silver bowl. "But there's no grimoire."

Alex shook his head. "I don't like this place. I have a bad feeling about it."

"But the image of the Goddess and the Hunter?" Avery said. "Surely these are good symbols?"

"They should be, but I just can't shake this feeling," he said. His dark eyes looked troubled, almost hooded in the light.

Reuben's face had taken on an almost fanatical gleam. "How long do you think our family used this place for?"

"It must have been built at the same time as the mausoleum, so maybe a couple of hundred years until the Witchfinder General scared them off?" Avery ventured.

Reuben traced the carvings with his hands. "Maybe they continued on their own after your families hid their grimoires."

Avery looked at Alex, concerned. "Do you think all of our families met here together at one point?"

He shrugged. "I think so. It's big enough."

As Avery walked around the room, she realised there were narrow channels cut into the floor, leading towards the altar, and lined with a dark stain. Her heart almost missed a beat. "Oh, crap. Is that old blood?"

Alex dropped to his hands and knees to examine it more closely. He sighed. "It looks like it." He looked up at Reuben, who was still examining the altar. "Reuben, let's get out of here."

He turned. "My grimoire is still in here somewhere."

"You don't know that."

"I do," he insisted. "I'm not leaving 'til we find it." He turned away again, his shoulders set.

Alex stood and moved next to Avery. "Let's make this quick," he said softly.

A dark feeling of dread crept up Avery's back. It felt like something was in the room with them. Reuben was whispering spells at the front by the altar as he traced the carvings, desperate to find another mechanism. While he examined the altar, Avery and Alex walked the perimeter of the room, examining the walls for any hint of an opening or a hidden door. The rest of the walls were plain, the thick stones and their fine joins the only marks, other than a couple of small alcoves with old candles in them.

They joined Reuben, who had walked over to the devil's trap positioned in the far corner of the room. Crude runes were cut in the floor in front of it. Despite the bright orange light from the lanterns, Avery felt as if the room was growing darker.

"I think the runes are a summoning spell," Reuben said, dropping to his knees.

"Great, let's not say it, then," Avery said, wishing she was outside in the fresh air.

"Makes you wonder if they summoned a demon regularly though, doesn't it?" he asked, running his hand across the runes. "Maybe it was their own personal demon?"

"For small personal requests?" Alex said, sarcasm dripping from his voice.

"Why else have a devil's trap in the floor?"

Avery turned away towards the altar again, wondering what her ancestors got up to in here. She ran her hand across the engravings on the wall, trying to find comfort in the images of the Goddess and the Hunter and failing. Her gaze dropped to the floor and she saw the channels stained with old blood narrowing to join at the base of the wall, a shallow stone pool just visible before it disappeared under the wall. She felt her breath catch, and the others turned to her.

"What?" Alex asked, at her side immediately.

"Look," she pointed, curious now despite her misgivings. "There's the edge of a shallow bowl—it disappears under the wall. Maybe the wall moves back?"

"Maybe we need blood to move it back," Reuben suggested.

Both Alex and Avery looked at him in alarm, but before they could stop them, he had pulled a small knife out of his pocket and slashed across his palm, just as Alex had done for his spell.

"No, wait!" Alex said, leaping to stop Reuben. "We don't know what it will do."

But it was too late. Reuben crouched down, squeezing his palm, and a bright stream of blood dropped onto the channels and into the shallow bowl.

Avery stepped back, alarmed.

For a few seconds, nothing happened.

"Maybe it needs more blood," Reuben muttered as he repeatedly squeezed his palm to increase the blood flow.

Alex moved closer to Avery, pulling her back into the centre of the room. "Reuben, enough."

There was a loud *click* as the entire wall cracked in half right down the middle, a previously invisible vertical line appearing in the wall between the Goddess and the Hunter. The walls swung back, hinged like doors, and the almost silent *shush* of the mechanism sent chills up Avery's spine.

Beyond the door was a small room, an altar up against the far wall, cast in shadows. They could now see the whole of the stone bowl in the floor. Leading from it, another thicker stone channel led to the second altar.

Avery sent the witch light into the space and gasped when she saw a dimensional doorway carved onto the stone wall at the back, above the second altar. "Not another one!"

"Please tell me your blood isn't running that far," Alex said, his tone abrupt as he addressed Reuben.

"No," Reuben said, throwing an annoyed glance back over his shoulder to Alex. "My palm does not produce rivers of blood!"

"Good. Watch where you drip. We don't want to accidentally open that thing."

But Reuben was already wrapping a portion of his t-shirt around his injured hand. He stepped around the original altar that stood before the wall and went into the smaller room, letting out a short cry of joy. "The grimoire."

Alex and Avery tentatively followed Reuben and saw a small wooden box on the altar, and resting in it was a thick, leather-bound book. Reuben reached forward for it, but Alex shouted, "Stop! Let me."

Reuben stopped mid-reach and frowned at Alex.

"Let's not get your blood on anything else," Alex said, stepping past him and checking the book from all angles before he reached in and lifted it up.

"Sorry, you're right," Reuben muttered. "Is it my grimoire?"

"Sure looks like it," Alex said, turning the first few pages carefully.

Avery saw some objects on the altar and frowned as she tried to identify them. There was what looked like small bone, and maybe a ring, placed together, and next to it a bundle of hair. "Oh, crap!" she said, realising what she was looking at. "That's a finger bone!"

The others turned quickly. "Where?" Alex asked.

"On the altar." She picked the ring up and held it under the light. It was made of gold and it had a large, red stone set into it; the ring was large, undoubtedly made for a man. She dropped it back onto the altar, grimacing.

"Let's get out of here," Reuben said, his bravado from earlier long gone. "We've got what we came for."

As they stepped out of the hidden room, the doors closed softly behind them with a whisper that seemed to come from beyond the grave. Avery desperately hoped they wouldn't need to return here, but had a horrible feeling they would.

11

Alex and Avery followed Reuben down the driveway of Greenlane Manor, the gravel crunching beneath the wheels of Alex's Alfa Romeo. At this hour the grounds were deserted, and the only light came from the window by the huge front door.

"What did you think of the hidden room?" Alex asked her. His face cast mostly in shadow looked grim.

"I hated it. It was oppressive and threatening." She hesitated for a second, wondering if she really wanted to voice what she thought, but this was Alex, and she knew he'd probably feel the same. "It's clear that blood magic, dark magic, was done there, and it worries me that Reuben doesn't seem to care too much."

"It worries me, too. I think his need to avenge Gil may be blinding him to some things."

"And he's inexperienced with magic," Avery added. "I mean, he has power, certainly, but I think he's a bit naive about some magic and its implications. It sounds ridiculous, I know, considering we're what we're all being exposed to, and we're all using stronger magic than we have before, but at least we've been using it a lot longer."

Alex glanced across at her. "Well, he's lost Gil, and isn't really speaking to El, so we're going to have to keep an eye on him."

"And he's here with Alicia," Avery said, feeling her anxiety rise. "We still don't really know what she's up to."

"Reuben's not stupid, though. We need to trust him."

They rolled to a halt in the turning circle in front of the steps to the manor and followed Reuben as he crossed the huge, echoing entrance hall, leading them up the sweeping stairs to his suite of rooms on the top floor. He left the main lights off, and only a couple of lamps casting low light illuminated their way. Avery peeked through open doorways, noting that the furniture looked expensive and antique; it was a very glamorous house. She hadn't been in here for years, and had forgotten how grand it was. It had definitely been refurbished since her childhood.

Reuben's suite of rooms was on the second floor, overlooking the sea. They stepped into a small entrance hall and passed through it into a large sitting room. A small kitchen was located on the back wall, and a door led off to a bedroom, and another to a bathroom. It was nothing like Avery had imagined. She presumed Reuben would live in some sort of disaster of surfboards and shorts, with stuff everywhere, but instead it was all cream linen, dark grey walls, a slick sound system, and an enormous TV.

"You all right?" Reuben asked her, starting to laugh at her expression.

"It's not what I expected!"

He winked, "Not quite the surf dive you imagined?"

"No," she said, feeling embarrassed.

"That's because we have cleaners."

"Lucky you," Alex said, walking over to the window to look at the view. A pale sliver of moon illuminated the sea beyond the bottom of the garden, and Avery could hear the waves crashing against the shore. The glasshouse glinted on the lawn below, and a vision of the hidden passageway and Gil's death filled Avery's thoughts.

Reuben turned on some lamps, and with a flick of a switch, the curtains started to close, dispelling the darkness. He locked the door behind them, and then headed to the rear wall and a section of dark oak panelling. "What I'm about to show you must remain a secret," he said, very serious.

"Of course," Avery said, raising her eyebrow speculatively at Alex.

"Our family is very big on hidden doorways, passageways, and rooms within rooms," Reuben explained, releasing a mechanism which allowed a hidden door within the panel to pop out.

"You've got to be kidding me!" Avery exclaimed.

"We're at the far end of the house, and this passageway leads up to a section of the attic that is separate from the rest. I shared it with Gil, but he accessed it through another door."

They followed him down a long, narrow passage and then up a steep flight of stairs, all hidden in the narrow space between two walls, and then they went through another door and a section of crowded attic space stretched ahead of them.

The centre was dominated by a large table, covered in books. A selection of unmatched chairs were scattered around the place, all upholstered with old fading material. The floor was made of wide wooden planks, and shelves lined the end wall, along either side of a fireplace. There were no windows here at all, and on the far side of the room was another door. Gil's entrance, she presumed.

"How on Earth did you get the furniture in here?" Avery asked, looking around in amazement.

"One of our ancestors brought them in years ago, through that wall." He pointed to the main dividing wall that separated them from the rest of the attic. "And then they bricked it up again. From the other side it's impossible to see that there's anything here, and the attic space is so huge and full of crap, you don't even realise it's shorter than it should be."

"So this spans the width of the house?" Alex asked, walking around.

"Yes, and therefore big enough for our needs. My needs," he said, correcting himself. He placed the newly found grimoire on the table. "It's nice to finally put this where it should be."

He switched on a desk lamp and angled it over the book, and despite her increasing tiredness, Avery looked at the book with excitement.

The cover, like the others, was made of thick old leather, but unlike the others was a dark blue. The arcane symbol for water was embossed on the front, an upside-down triangle, and on the first page was the usual list of all the witches who had used the grimoire before. Reuben ran his hand across it and closed his eyes briefly. He looked incredibly sad. "Gil should be here for this."

"Yes, he should. I'm so sorry he's not," Avery agreed, moving closer to Reuben and resting her hand on his arm. "How *are* you, Reuben?"

"I'm fine. I just want to find Faversham and kill him, that's all."

"There'll be ways to deal with him." She glanced at Alex concerned. "Is Alicia back here?"

Reuben concentrated on the grimoire as he spoke. "No, but she's coming back soon. She texted me to say she'd like to stay here until she's found somewhere else to live."

"And you're okay with that?"

"Of course I am," he said impatiently. "It was her home. I've told her she can take as long as she wants."

Avery glanced up at Alex, and he shook his head. Now was not the time to ambush Reuben by questioning Alicia's loyalties.

Alex changed the subject. "What sorts of spells are in there?"

Reuben sighed as he turned the pages, "I'm not sure—the writing is so hard to read!" He sounded exasperated, and a bit emotional.

"It's been a long night, Reuben," Alex said. "You should rest and read this tomorrow. We'll go and leave you to it, but would you mind if we checked the back first? To see if the hidden spell is in yours, too?"

Reuben shook himself. "Yeah, of course."

They doused the electric lights and produced a witch light that cast a pale, silvery glow over the attic. Reuben turned to the end of the grimoire, and there on the back pages was a spell, the lines of incantation headed: *Part Four, To Suspend in Water*. Avery felt dizzy, and wasn't sure if she was pleased or horrified. Like the others, it was clearly incomplete.

"Just need your grimoire then, Avery," Alex said, "and the spell will be complete."

12

Tuesday passed in a blur of work. Avery found it hard to concentrate, her head swimming with all the new information about the hidden room beneath the Jackson's mausoleum and discovering another part of the spell. She found her mind often drifting back to the map hidden in the old book upstairs, and a couple of times customers had had to repeat questions.

Sally had noticed her distraction, and over mid-afternoon coffee and cake taken in a break between customers, she asked, "Are you okay, Avery?"

Avery took a bite of her slice of coffee and walnut cake, thinking she could eat the entire cake in one sitting. "This cake is fantastic, Sally."

"Cheers, I made it last night, but stop avoiding the question! You're so distracted today."

Avery looked at her guiltily. "I know, sorry, I have a lot on my mind. My life has become very confusing lately."

"Do you want to share?"

Avery took another bite of cake, and wondered if she should. Sally was a good friend, and she valued her opinion, but she also had no idea about the extent of magic in White Haven. It was too dangerous to say much about it. "I'd love to, but it's too complicated. Things are very weird at the moment, and I think it's best if I say nothing for now."

Sally watched her for a second, and then nodded. "Fair enough, if you're sure. But keep safe. I feel whatever you're up to is dangerous."

"Have you still got your hex bag for protection?" Avery asked, with a flash of worry.

Sally reached into her blouse and pulled out the small bag, which she'd placed on a silver chain. "Right here."

"Good. I'll make sure Dan's got his, too."

"Will our other friends be okay, Avery, and my family?" Sometimes Avery was surprised by how perceptive Sally was.

"Yeah, I'm sure they will be. It's you and Dan who are more vulnerable, but don't ask me any more. I can't say." It was improbable that the Favershams would attack them directly; it was much more likely that they'd be caught in the crossfire of whatever magical war was taking place.

Sally nodded, seemingly reassured. "I'll be out back if you need me."

As she was locking up for the night, Avery received a text from Briar inviting her to her house at 6:30 p.m. *Newton's got news*, she'd sent enigmatically. *And don't eat, I'll feed you.*

Avery wound her way through the narrow streets of White Haven, enjoying the early evening sunshine. Locals and tourists alike were strolling the streets, heading to restaurants and bars, and a few shops were open late, enjoying the influx of tourists that the fine weather had brought.

Even in the middle of town, Avery could smell the sea, and the gulls wheeled overhead, their raucous cries echoing around the streets. Lately, Avery viewed the town with fresh eyes. She'd always taken its old buildings and history for granted, but now she felt she was part of its history. She could feel the past stretching its tendrils into the present. She noticed how the buildings from the different centuries all jostled together in a pleasing mix of styles, and she noticed how the town moved from one century to the next in the space of a few feet. It was exhilarating. She loved this place, and there was no way she was leaving, or letting the Favershams dictate what she would do. Despite the fact that she now knew more than she ever had, she still thought there was something else they had yet to find out, something that would reveal the true reason for Octavia's binding and Faversham's attack on Helena.

She turned onto Briar's street, a snaggy lane that stretched up the hill. The pavements were narrow, and the houses had tiny front gardens. She turned up the path and rang the bell, and then heard Briar call, "It's open."

Briar's front door opened straight into the low-ceilinged living room, where a massive old fireplace dominated the room. The space was filled with a comfortable sofa and armchairs, with bookcases on either side of the fireplace. A door at the rear led through to the kitchen, and Briar called again, "Come through, Avery."

The kitchen was small but packed with cupboards and efficiently organised. Briar stood at the counter, chopping salad.

"How did you know it was me?" Avery asked, wondering if Briar had hidden cameras installed somewhere.

Briar grinned. Her hair was wound on her head in a messy ponytail, and she wore a long, loose dress with a belt around it. Her feet were bare and she had painted her nails bright green. "I sensed you—you have a different energy than the others. You're all unique. Haven't you noticed?"

"I haven't, actually." Avery confessed, feeling she was missing something.

"My grimoire talks all about grounding, the earth, and energy signatures," she explained. "It's so much more than just a grimoire!" She grinned and it lit up her face.

"That makes sense. I saw auras when I spirit-walked with Alex, and they're different."

Briar concentrated on mixing the salad together. "I've been practising feeling the energy through the earth. I'm getting better—I feel my customers now before they've even entered the shop. I've started to pick up on moods, too." She stopped for a second and looked at her. "I can feel you and Alex—wow, you two!"

Avery flushed and opened the bottle of wine she'd brought with her, wondering how much to say, and then realised that their relationship really wasn't a secret to anyone. She looked at Briar's expectant face. "Yes, we have a *thing*. It's great so far, but I'm not sure how long it will last."

"You have trust issues. It's quite obvious he adores you."

Avery felt embarrassed and shocked. *Is that what others saw?* "He does not *adore* me! And if he does, he probably won't for long."

Briar rolled her eyes. "Stop it! El's right, the lady's man thing is an act. He's just a flirt—it means nothing."

Avery felt a flood of warmth spreading through her. It didn't matter how often people said it, she still doubted Alex could like her so much that it would last, but it was still good to hear. She swiftly changed the subject to avoid potential embarrassment. "And what about you and Newton?"

Briar turned away to the oven and shrugged. "I don't know. We're just friends."

"Now who's being coy!"

Briar pulled a bubbling, cheesy-topped lasagne out of the oven, and its rich scent flooded the kitchen. "Anyway, El's here."

Within seconds the front door opened and El came in, and they had barely said hello when Alex, Newton, and Reuben followed a few minutes later. Reuben glanced at El, but she looked away. Newton was out of his suit and again in jeans and a casual shirt. He nodded his hellos to everyone, his gaze lingering on Briar.

Alex, however, gave Avery a grin and a wink, and her heart raced. He wore his usual faded jeans and an old Led Zeppelin t-shirt, and his dark hair was loose. He plonked a six-pack of beer down on the bench. "Smells good, Briar. Cheers for cooking."

"My pleasure. I've set the table out back." She nodded towards the small lean-to sunroom at the back of the house. "Have a seat, and I'll bring everything through."

"I'll help," Newton said, immediately finding a tray.

Avery grinned and carried her bottle of wine into the sunroom, smiling at the ordered chaos. The sunroom stretched the length of the house, and a long wooden table ran down the centre, surrounded by old cane chairs heaped with mismatched cushions of stripes, patterns, and flowers. The table was laid with plates and glasses of different designs, but everything worked harmoniously. Plants filled the corners, and a small desk covered in papers was against the far wall. A small, riotous garden was out the back, planted around a tiny paved area, and the double doors to the patio stood wide open, letting in the warm evening air.

Avery sat at the far end of the table at the back, looking out over the garden, and Alex followed her out, sitting on her right, while Reuben sat opposite her. El sat next to Alex, as far from Reuben as she could get in this small place, and ignored him as much as possible.

Anxious to break the awkwardness, Avery said, "I love Briar's house. I've never been in it before."

Reuben nodded absentmindedly, and El answered, "Yeah, it's very Briar. Tiny garden, though—that's why she has an allotment."

"I'll have to visit it one day," Avery said thoughtfully. "I'm sure her new grimoire couldn't make her a better gardener, though."

"Any luck finding yours?" Reuben asked.

"No. It's infuriating. I've examined the map a thousand times, and I still can't work out where it is." She sipped her wine, wishing she wasn't the only one left to find her grimoire. *What if she couldn't ever find it?*

"I'll come round tomorrow evening, and we'll try again," Alex said.

Newton and Briar came out carrying the salad, lasagne, and garlic bread, and Avery inhaled the rich scents greedily. She realised she was starving, and helped herself to a liberal portion.

"Well, I have good news, sort of, to share," Newton began. "I've managed to find out quite a bit about the Favershams."

"And is it good news or bad?" Alex asked.

"Mostly bad." He sighed. "Look, before I start, you need to understand that while I was told about *my role*, I didn't really believe it. It sounded crazy, although my parents were insistent that it was real—are insistent, in fact. And of course now I know they're right."

The others nodded and El said, "It's okay, go on. We get it."

"I'll start with my old family records. The Favershams are definitely on my enemy list, and it started back during the witch trials when my ancestor, Peter Newton, was made to hang Helena because of the Witchfinder General and the Favershams. He felt so powerless that he vowed that it would never happen again. He started keeping tabs on the family, and realised they were rotten and corrupt. He made it his business to know what had happened, and to discover the

113

truth of their witchcraft. Most of the families—your families—left White Haven after Helena's death, but he spoke to Helena's brother-in-law, just before he fled with her children and his own family. He told Peter what had happened with Octavia. He didn't reveal all the details of why, though—he probably didn't know. Peter felt strongly enough, and was worried enough about the implications of it all, that he passed it on.

"So, odd things happened from time to time, but eventually things settled down. Nothing particularly bad happened for decades. The witches left, the Favershams continued to build their empire, and then your families returned and kept a very low profile. And from what I understand, never knew my family knew about them."

"You watched us from a distance," Alex deduced.

"Pretty much. And of course, doubt set in, about everything—although, it was dutifully passed on. There haven't been any specific incidents in recent years—other than with Reuben's great-great-whatever uncle years ago. Addison, more than anyone in years, decided to look for the grimoires. It wasn't enough for him to let sleeping dogs lie. He wanted the grimoires and the power they contained—" he held up a hand to stop any questions. "I don't know why— my family records don't describe those details—we're watchers, remember. But there was enough activity for my great-great grandfather to be aware that *something* was happening. Anyway, Addison started the search, and the Favershams found out. They threatened him and his family. It seems that Addison had found one of the grimoires, and they knew about it. In order to protect his family, he did what we all now know—he faked their deaths and disappeared, under the cover of black magic and a blood sacrifice. Something designed to scare anyone off searching in future.

And knowledge of the grimoire disappeared with him. Your family, Reuben," Newton glanced at him, "continued the lie. Or should have."

Avery groaned as everything dropped into place. "But Lottie shared what she knew with Anne, and Anne was charged with keeping the secret—and the hidden grimoire."

Newton nodded. "Lottie was of a younger generation, but she found out what her uncle had done, and decided it was too big and too important to hide."

"So, they waited until things had calmed down and the story had been forgotten," Avery said, nodding. "How did your family find out, Newton?"

"My great-grandfather was also in the police, and had to investigate the disappearance. He found out what happened, and also played along—but left records of the truth for us." He shrugged. "As I told you the other night, it seemed crazy to me. I barely believed it, and didn't really read the records properly. I've known about you all of course, and your magical history and abilities, but again, I thought it was superstitious nonsense. I didn't even believe the grimoire stuff—I barely knew what it meant. It was only when that woman died on the moors that I really started to believe—it was obvious that wasn't normal. And then you told me about the grimoires the other night, and it all came flooding back—my *other* job became a reality."

"It's like Chinese whispers, isn't it?" Briar said. "Things get forgotten and distorted over time, until we can barely sort the truth from fiction."

"And it started over 400 years ago," Reuben pointed out. "No wonder it sounded crazy."

"But what about that vision you had, in your flat?" Alex asked Avery.

She frowned. "I must have been picking up on the Favershams and Caspian, the blood magic that had been used, and made the wrong association."

"Well," Newton continued after a mouthful of food, "I've checked the family out. Sebastian, as we know is head of the family and the CEO of Kernow Shipping. Caspian is his son and head of finance, and his daughter, Estelle, is head of overseas investments. He has a couple of nephews called," he consulted his notebook, which made him look super official, "Hamish and Rory, and Sebastian's brother, Rupert, is also on the board—he's their father. I have no idea about their magical abilities, of course, but it seems prudent to think they have them."

"So the dark-haired woman who attacked us at the church was Estelle?" Avery asked.

Newton nodded.

Alex narrowed his eyes, "Any suspicion of anything dodgy?"

"No, other than that they're rich and like a say in *everything*. They have their fingers in many, many pies in Harecombe. They're Council members, on the arts committee, benefactors to the art gallery and museum…" Newton rolled his eyes and took a mouthful of lasagne. "You name it, they do it."

"I loathe them even more than I did already," Briar said as she picked at her salad.

Newton paused and looked at Reuben for a second, a flash of concern breaking his police manner. "I've found out that Alicia is related to them, too."

Reuben's head shot up, and he stared at Newton. "*Gil's* Alicia?"

"Yes."

"How?"

"She's another cousin, from Sebastian's younger sister, Honoria."

They all fell silent, and Avery wondered what Reuben was thinking right now. He looked shocked, then surprised, and then finally put his fork down. "Sorry, I'm really confused. Does she work with them? Because I thought she had her own interior design business? And did Gil know?"

"I've no idea what Gil knew, Reuben, but I doubt it. You didn't. And no, she's not part of their business—well, not an obvious one. She's not listed on their company records. It seems she really is an interior designer, and a busy one. She's very popular with some very rich families all across Cornwall, and that includes hotels."

Reuben looked white beneath his deep tan, and he pushed his plate away. "Did she have anything to do with his death?"

Newton looked apologetic and ran his hand through his hair. "I don't know, and I'm not sure I can find out. But you may be able to."

Reuben looked at Avery accusingly. "You were asking me about Alicia, in the caves, just before he died. Did you know something?"

Avery had a sudden jolt of panic and wondered how much she should say, but she felt Alex's leg nudge her own gently, and she realised she had to voice her doubts. "I didn't know anything, no, of course not, I'd have said so. But, I did wonder how Faversham seemed to know so much, and it struck me that maybe Alicia knew more than Gil realised— she did live with him. With both of you."

Reuben looked at her wide-eyed with shock. "But you didn't say a thing!" He sounded incredulous. "I've been living with her ever since Gil died. The grimoire is there *now!*"

He scraped his chair back and stood up, ready to leave, and Avery rose too, as if to stop him. "No, wait! I didn't know! I could have been wrong—*we could still be wrong!*"

"I need to see her. *Now!*" He edged around the table, making for the door into the kitchen. Newton stood, authority emanating from him. "No. Sit down, Reuben. We need to think this through."

"I don't need to think anything through. Butt out, Newton."

Alex also leapt to his feet and stopped Reuben at the door, his hand on Reuben's arm. "Reuben, as much as I hate to agree with Newton, he's right. We need to have a plan. She could be hiding a heap of magic."

Reuben glared at him and shrugged his hand off. "While I'm standing here arguing with you, my grimoire could be gone and the woman responsible for Gil's death is strolling around my house! Get out of my way. I don't want to hit you, but I will."

"Nice. Resorting to violence again," El said, looking at Reuben with a mixture of sorrow and anger.

Reuben paused for a second, shocked, and then continued relentlessly. "Excuse me for having feelings!"

All of El's anxiety and anger came bursting out after days of simmering resentment. "We all have feelings, Reuben. We don't have to hurt our *friends*, though!"

The magical energy in the room had shot up by then, and as well as feeling wind stirring around her, Avery noticed a flicker of flames in El's hands. *Wow. Things got ugly really quickly.*

Alex was trying hard to keep his cool. "Trust in your magic, Reuben. You have a hidden room, and it's hidden with magic, too—isn't it?"

"Yes," Reuben nodded, "of course."

"Then it should be fine."

"I'm not taking that risk. And I need to know if Alicia betrayed Gil," Reuben said, and he pushed around Alex and into the kitchen, slamming the door behind him.

"We can't let him do this alone, whatever he says," Alex said, turning to follow him. "Newton, come on. We need to stop him before he does something stupid."

"He's right though, Alex, we have to find out about Alicia." Avery reasoned, feeling the need to defend Reuben. "Caspian's already got away with killing him, and for Alicia to get away with betraying Gil as well is too much. I'm coming, too."

Briar looked at El, who remained seated, her face like stone. "I'll stay here with El."

"You don't have to babysit me, Briar."

"Of course I don't, but I'm staying anyway." Briar looked up at the others. "Go on, and stay safe."

13

Newton's sleek BMW sedan raced down the lanes, but despite the fact that they were only minutes behind Reuben, he was already lost to sight. They arrived with a screech of brakes and a splatter of gravel in front of Greenlane Manor and found Reuben's car abandoned and the front door wide open.

They ran up the steps and into the reception hall, and then hesitated. It was dusk and a couple of lights were on, but the rest of the house was in darkness.

"Where the hell are they?" Newton said, trying to contain his anger. All the way to the house they had debated over what to do, but as Newton said, you can't legally accuse someone of black magic and be taken seriously. He darted into the adjoining rooms and shouted, "Reuben!"

Silence surrounded them. They fanned out, checking the ground floor, but every room was eerily empty and extremely tidy.

"Where's her suite of rooms? They must be in there," Avery reasoned, itching to release some of her pent-up energy, while trying to convince herself that Alicia could be completely innocent and just a grieving widow.

"Let's try upstairs, the opposite side from Reuben's rooms," Alex suggested, running up the stairs.

The first floor was in darkness, so they raced up the next flight, coming to a sudden halt as they saw a sliver of light coming from an open doorway, far down the corridor to their left.

They edged closer, Avery trying hard to catch her breath, and heard shouting. It was a woman's voice. "Don't be ridiculous, Reuben. You're scaring me, stop it!"

"Don't play the coy woman with me. You're related to the man who killed Gil, and I want to know what you had to do with it."

"No one killed Gil, it was an accident."

"Bullshit. I was there. He was killed by Caspian Faversham, your cousin. Now, tell me what you know, or I will blast you from the face of the Earth."

They all looked at each other in alarm, and then Newton pushed the door open and stepped in. "Reuben! Calm down."

Alex followed with Avery close behind, both of them stepping on either side of Newton, ready to attack if necessary.

Reuben and Alicia were standing in front of an unlit fireplace, a few feet between them. Alicia stepped back as they entered, fear etched across her face. Reuben towered over her, emphasising how small she was.

Reuben shouted, "Keep out of this—all of you."

Alicia looked as if she might retreat further and then thought better of it. She appealed to Newton. "He's gone mad! He's ranting about witches and magic. You're the detective—I demand you arrest him!"

"The thing is," Newton said, stepping closer, "I know you're related to the Faversham—a magical family—and I know the whole family has a grudge against White Haven. So, you need to prove to me you had nothing to do with Gil's death."

Her face drained of colour. "I may be related, but I have my own life, my own business. I was away when he died!"

"But you're not denying magic anymore, are you?" Newton countered.

Reuben rounded on her again. "He trusted you, Alicia! I trusted you! He hid his magic for years, and you didn't even share that with him! Why?"

"It was a part of my life I've stepped away from." Unexpectedly she stepped forward, appealing to Reuben. "You did, too, I know all about it. You know why that happens."

Avery reeled slightly at her admission. So she *did* have magical abilities. Avery watched her and wondered how true it was that she had abandoned it. Alicia's hands were flexing nervously, and Avery was convinced this was still an act. She'd do anything to stay in the house. Maybe she hadn't found the grimoire yet.

Reuben glared at her. "It would have broken Gil's heart. He loved you, and you lied to him for years!"

"He would have wanted me to practice, and I didn't want that."

Reuben was furious. "Bollocks. You liar. Ever since Avery was gifted that box, you have been betraying us. That bastard Caspian has threatened us, attacked us, and killed Gil. You are the only one who could have told him what we were doing!"

"No!" Alicia was pleading now, stepping back again, away from the fireplace. Reuben followed her, keeping only a couple of paces away, and Avery noticed her glancing towards the fireplace.

What was she doing? She seemed to be waiting for something.

And then a horrible thought struck Avery.

Demons.

As soon as she thought it, Reuben stepped right in front of the fireplace, his back to it as he shouted at Alicia, and instantaneously, with a horrendous snarl and smell of sulphur, a demon appeared, flames whirling around it. A long flame lashed at an unsuspecting Reuben.

Avery, however was prepared, her energy already gathered. It was as if she'd had a sixth sense of what would happen. She sent a powerful, targeted blast of air at Reuben, knocking him clean out of the way, and he flew backwards across the room, crashing into a glass-fronted cabinet.

Avery turned her attention to Alicia and sent a second blast right at her, taking her legs out from under her and throwing her into the path of the demon that had now stepped into the room, flames lashing out in all directions. Alicia screamed as she threw up her hands to protect herself.

A second demon appeared behind the first, and Avery glanced at Alex. He sent a powerful flash of energy, which seemed neither flame nor air, straight at the creature that'd just arrived, trying to unbalance it before it could attack. Newton ran to the far side of the room, pulling a dazed Reuben out of the broken glass.

Both demons stepped forward together, advancing on the room. Alicia was back on her feet, shouting something in a language Avery didn't understand, but she appeared to be trying to control the demons.

There was a spell Avery knew that she had never tried before, but it should work perfectly—if she understood the relationship between a witch and their demon correctly. As she uttered it, she felt mean, but it was either Alicia or them.

She had tried to kill Reuben, and if she had her way, they'd all be dead. This was no time for sentiment.

It was a spell to bind the tongue.

It was done in seconds. Alicia choked and gagged, and then turned with fury towards Alex and Avery, and then fury turned to fear and then terror as she clutched at her throat, trying to speak the words of command.

Alicia was far closer to the demons than anyone else, but Avery could feel their heat from across the room. Their lashing flames scorched everything they touched. But as Alicia fell silent, the demons stopped their advance and turned on her.

Alicia backed away, but Avery uttered another spell, and Alicia collapsed on the floor. The demons pounced.

They smothered Alicia in their burning grasp. Their voices—if that's what they even were—blood curdling in pitch. Gaping jaws revealed hundreds of tiny teeth, and Alicia disappeared within the dark folds of their nebulous bodies. She couldn't even scream.

Alex stepped forward and started an incantation. Avery recognised the spell they had used in the witch museum, or something similar. He was trying to banish them.

Avery joined him, holding his outstretched hand, adding her strength to his, and Reuben, who had now staggered to his feet, joined in on the other side. Newton, unable to help at all, moved behind them.

They repeated the spell after Alex, their voices growing in power, and the demons retreated, their forms becoming insubstantial. They stepped back into the fireplace, and with a thunderous clap, they disappeared, taking Alicia with them.

Soot poured down the chimney and billowed into the room.

The silence that followed seemed profound. The room was covered in long, black burn marks, parts of the rug smouldered, objects were broken, and the glass cabinet was smashed.

"Is everyone okay?" Alex asked, partially covering his face from the soot.

"I've got a massive burn on my arm and chest, but I think I'll survive," Newton said from behind them.

Avery whirled around and found Newton collapsed on the floor. His shirt was smoking, and parts of it had disintegrated where the flames had caught, burning his chest. She dropped to her knees, examining him. "We'll get you to Briar."

"I'm okay, really." His grey eyes were filled with pain, but he nodded towards Reuben.

Avery turned and found Reuben on his knees, too, crying shamelessly, tears pouring down his face. Alex crouched next to him, his hand on his shoulder. "I'm sorry, Reuben. This just sucks."

Reuben looked past Alex to Avery, and the look in his eyes almost broke her heart. "Thank you for that, Avery. You saved me—I'll never forget it."

She started to well up, too. "I wasn't about to lose you too, Reuben." She looked back at Newton. "What have I done? I've killed Alicia! Will you arrest me?"

He shook his head. "No, you didn't. Her own demons killed her."

Panic flooded through her. "But I made her powerless. I caused it."

"You were a bloody genius," Alex said, looking at her admiringly. "You saved us all."

"Let's just agree it was a group effort. You banished the demons." She wiped away a tear. "How are we going to explain Alicia's death?"

"There's no body," Newton said, wincing with pain.

"But she's gone. Forever."

Newton shook his head, "Leave it with me. I'm here as a friend, not a policeman. I don't have to write any reports. Easiest thing is to say that she's disappeared. But pain is interfering with my reason right now, so if we could go…"

"Of course!" Avery leapt to her feet, and helped pull Newton up. "Are we all going back to Briar's?"

Alex looked at Reuben. "Are we?"

Reuben shook his head, and gestured to the smouldering rug. "No. I'll stay here. I need to make sure the place doesn't burn down and check on my grimoire—and I just want to be alone right now."

"I disagree. I think El should be with you," Alex said, clearly worried about leaving Reuben alone.

Reuben wiped his face with his hand. "I think we both know I've completely messed that up."

Alex looked at Avery and Newton. "I'll stay here for a while. Is there a car I can borrow later, Reuben?"

"Sure. You can use Gil's. It's still in the garage. But, honestly, go now."

Alex stood firm. "No. I'm staying here. I want to make sure those demons don't come back."

Reuben looked relieved, despite his protestations. "Cheers, mate."

Alex had a quiet word with them outside the room. "Speak to El, will you? He needs her."

"Of course," Avery said, and she kissed him on the cheek, thinking how adorable he was sometimes.

14

Briar and El were still in the sunroom when the pair arrived. The table had been cleared, and they sat quietly talking over a glass of wine. Briar leapt up as soon as they entered, Avery supporting Newton. His burns were more severe than she'd initially thought, and although she had used a spell to help reduce the pain, they needed Briar's help.

"By the goddess! What happened?" Briar asked, rushing over and helping Newton into a deep wicker seat filled with cushions.

"Demons," Avery said.

"Where are Alex and Reuben?" El asked, her voice strained.

"They're fine. Alicia is not." She explained quickly what had happened, and Briar gathered her herbs and started to treat Newton, easing his shirt off. A very angry burn stretched across his chest and down his arm, the skin already blistered. Newton lay back, breathing deeply, his face white with pain.

Avery sat next to El, leaving Briar to concentrate. "El, I know you're mad at him, but Reuben's really down. Gil's dead, Alicia betrayed them both, and he's hurting. Really hurting. He needs you. And you know he didn't mean to hurt you."

El's pretty face crumpled and her bravado disappeared as she started to cry. "I love him, Avery, but he really hurt my feelings." She looked at her, desperate and confused. "What am I going to do? I miss him like crazy."

"He misses you, too. He hates himself for what happened at the beach—I know he does. Go to him. Please. You two will work it out."

El nodded and exhaled deeply. "You're right. We're not kids. I'm going now."

"You okay to drive?"

"Fine. I've only had one drink." She stood, and then turned at the door. "Thanks, girls, you're both amazing."

***

It was another hour before Alex arrived, and Avery and Briar were talking quietly. Newton had gone to bed in the spare room, after having a strong herbal draft to help him sleep.

Alex grabbed a beer from the fridge and sat down, his face drawn. "The grimoire's gone."

"Reuben's?" Avery asked, her stomach churning already.

"No!" Briar cried, simultaneously.

"Yep." He took a long drink. "Reuben is a mess right now. He's veering between anger and grief. He's on a massive emotional roller coaster. Thank the gods El turned up, because I'm crap at that sort of thing."

"Not true," Briar shot back. "You're not a Neanderthal, Alex."

He gave a sad smile. "Well, I think El's comforting arms are far more attractive than my pats on the shoulder."

"Are they okay?" Avery asked.

"They will be. I left them to it. We searched the house first, just in case Alicia had secreted it somewhere to give to

Caspian. But it's either really well hidden, or he's already got it."

"She knew where the hidden attic was all along, and was powerful enough to break Reuben's protection. I know this sounds horrible, but I'm glad those demons took her. What a bitch." Avery wondered what she was turning into to think such a thing. "Magic karma is going to hit me where it hurts I think."

"No, it's not," Briar said, soothingly. "You acted to protect others. And I'm sorry I wasn't there to help—I felt I should stay with El."

"You did the right thing," Avery reassured her.

Alex looked thoughtful. "So, Alicia's responsible for the demons then, not Caspian?"

"It looks that way," Avery said. "But who knows, it could be a family trait. I'm sure he had a hand in some of it."

"What are we going to do?" Briar asked, appealing to both of them. "We can't let them get away with it."

Alex stood up abruptly. "I don't know, but we'll think of something. I'm starving, and I can't think on an empty stomach. Any food left? I didn't really eat much earlier—sorry, Briar."

"No problem. It's still warming in the oven. And," she added, raising her voice as he headed into the kitchen, "I have fudge cake in the fridge. Well, some of it. El had rather a large slice."

"Ooh, yes please," Avery said, brightening up. "You are a domestic goddess, Briar. You heal, garden, and cook."

"I'll bring it in," Alex shouted back. He returned with a bowl of lasagne and the cake on a plate with a knife. "Brilliant. So, I think we should do what they least expect and go to the Faversham nest."

"Really? Is that wise?" Briar questioned, alarmed.

Alex swallowed a mouthful of food. "Yep. What are they going to do? We'll be in their public offices. They can't attack us there, or summon demons."

"Well, that's true," Briar agreed.

"I'll either see Caspian or his father, whoever's there. I don't care which. It's time we talked. I want that grimoire back."

"Well, I'm coming, too," Avery declared immediately, through a mouthful of cake.

"What are you going to say?" Briar asked, perplexed.

"I don't know," Alex said, frowning. "But I'll think of something. This has got to stop. We're even now—one down on either side. I think that's enough, don't you?"

"Are you taking Newton?"

"No. This is unofficial—Newton shouldn't get involved."

***

Kernow Shipping was based in an old warehouse across from the harbour at Harecombe, and had been tastefully modernised with large glass windows and solid wooden doors.

Harecombe itself was a larger town than White Haven, with a bigger harbour, more hotels, but far less atmosphere— although Avery conceded that it was still very pretty.

She sat next to Alex in his car; the roof was down and a warm breeze ruffled their hair. They were in a public car park, watching a few people as they pottered around the bay, enjoying the summer sun.

"I presume their big ships dock elsewhere," Avery said speculatively.

"Falmouth," Alex said. "I checked. But they keep their base here. Handily close to us," he added sarcastically.

"So, what now?" She looked at him. "You've been suspiciously quiet on our plan of attack."

"That's because it's really basic." He flashed her a knowing smile. "I'm going to march in, befuddle the receptionist, and introduce ourselves to daddy."

"Is that *too* simple? We are marching into enemy witch central."

"And they employ lots of non-magical people. They'll be limited in what they can do," he reasoned. "I'll do the talking—you're my wingman."

"Cheers! Don't trust me to speak?" Avery was slightly offended, but also quite excited to be Alex's wingman.

"Of course I do, but you're my silent aggressor."

"I thought we were planning on calling a truce—to try for a 'lay our cards on the table' sort of thing."

"Yes, *we are*, I'm just not sure so sure they will want to, though."

They exited the car and sauntered over to the warehouse. Once inside the wide lobby, the outside noise disappeared in the hush of the expensive, double-glazed, carpeted area. Large framed paintings were on the walls, huge potted plants flanked the entrance and the lifts, and two receptionists sat behind a gleaming oak counter.

Both receptionists were in their mid-thirties, and one looked up as Alex leaned on the counter, flashing his most charming smile. Avery stood just behind, scanning the lifts and the entrance. Apart from them, the lobby was empty.

"Hi, I have an appointment to see Mr Sebastian Faversham."

The receptionist looked at the screen for a moment, and then said, "I'm sorry, Mr Faversham doesn't have any appointments booked this morning."

"I think you'll find I'm booked in," Alex said, still smiling.

She looked at the screen again and then looked up, confused, "Oh yes, I don't know how I could have missed that. What did you say your name was? I'll buzz you up."

"No need," Alex said, and Avery felt the fizz of magic as he glamoured her.

The receptionist next to her looked puzzled and went to intervene, and then she smiled vacantly, too. "So sorry for the confusion."

"No problem, ladies. Remind me which floor?"

"The top one, corner office. All the senior partners are on that floor." Her eyes were slightly gazed and Avery knew that once they left, both of them would forget that the conversation ever happened.

"Excellent," Alex said, smiling.

They hurried over to the lifts and waited impatiently for one to arrive.

"I feel I'm in the dragon's lair," Avery said, her senses alert and watchful.

"Fun, isn't it?" Alex said, flashing her a grin.

"You're nuts."

"I know."

As the lift arrived and the doors swished open, Avery saw a figure coming through the main doors. As they stepped inside, he looked up and caught her eye. *Caspian.* As the doors closed on them, she just had time to enjoy the look of shock on his face.

"Oops, we may have company. Caspian's here."

"Good. The more the merrier." Alex muttered a small spell and Avery felt the lift speed up until they arrived at the top with a thump.

"Alex!" Avery said, trying to keep her balance.

"Come on, Ave, time is of the essence. I want to see Caspian burst in on us and try to smooth his father's very ruffled feathers."

"We might be dead before then."

"Oh ye of little faith," Alex said under his breath as he exited the lift.

The first thing they saw was a stunning view of the harbour through a long window, directly opposite the lift. In front of it was a small reception area, with a gleaming white counter and a large vase of flowers. The heady aroma of lilies swirled around them. A couple of chairs and a table were placed in front of it, a waiting area no doubt for visitors to the board members' offices.

On their left, a row of offices led to a large window at the other end, their doors open, but on the right was a small, open plan office area where two secretaries sat, working at computers. They looked up briefly and went back to their work. Avery felt reassured. Witnesses hopefully meant they wouldn't die here.

This time, the lady seated behind the main desk was older. She had silver-grey hair tied back in a neat chignon, and she wore a very lovely pale lilac silk dress. She looked alarmed as they crossed towards her, and rose to her feet. Avery presumed their casual dress was not something she was used to seeing on visitors to the senior partners' floor.

"May I help you?" she asked dismissively, as if that was the last thing she wanted to do.

"We're here to see Seb. I understand he's in the corner office—we won't disturb you."

Avery stifled a giggle. *Seb?* Alex was really pushing his luck.

"I beg your pardon? Do you have an appointment?"

"Of course I do," Alex said as he leaned close to her, and again, Avery recognised a whiff of a glamour spell.

Avery wondered if the receptionist up here had any magical powers, because that might complicate things, but instead, her demeanour softened and she said, "Of course, the end office on the left."

As soon as they were out of sight they ran to the end of the corridor, hoping no one else would emerge from the other rooms, and found themselves in front of two offices, one bearing Sebastian's name, and one that said *Personal Assistant* on it. The door to his PA was ajar, and they could hear the muted murmur of a phone conversation.

Avery felt as if Caspian might arrive at any moment, but before she could say anything, Alex didn't hesitate. He softly closed the PA's door and locked it with a whispered spell, and then threw open Sebastian's door, saying, "Good morning, Faversham! So pleased to finally meet you."

Faversham's corner office was enormous, as was his desk, and the man behind it was imposing. Avery estimated he was in his late fifties or early sixties, but he looked fit. He was slim and handsome, with a full head of silvery hair.

He looked up in shock and then rose to his feet, his eyes narrowing. "Mr Bonneville."

"Mr Faversham."

"And Ms Hamilton."

Avery nodded, but remained silent, standing just behind and to Alex's right, where she could see the corridor behind. She scanned the room, but other than beautiful pieces of antique furnishings, Sebastian was alone.

He regained his composure swiftly. "So, you're here to talk about the terms of your surrender?"

Alex laughed. "No, we're here to talk about the return of the grimoire."

Sebastian also laughed; a dry, unpleasant noise with a smile that didn't reach his eyes. Cold eyes, Avery decided, lacking any warmth at all. "It's good to see you have a sense of humour, Mr Bonneville. Or shall I call you Alex?"

"You can call me whatever you want. I just want the grimoire."

Sebastian stepped around his desk and walked across the carpeted room towards them. He was as stealthy and as self-possessed as a cat.

As he approached, Avery noticed movement from the corner of her eye. Caspian came into view from the corridor outside. He caught her eye and paused for a second, and for a brief moment, Avery was confused by his reaction, and she hesitated, too. He looked worried, not angry. His eyes darted to her and then to the room, and as he stepped through the doorway, Avery called out, "Alex, we have company."

Rather than looking pleased, Sebastian scowled at his son. "Where have you been?"

"Seeking some answers," Caspian replied enigmatically.

Alex stepped aside, and they faced each other in a standoff, all four of them poised and ready to attack.

Sebastian thought for a moment and then gestured to some chairs and a table in the corner of his office. "Let's sit and be civilised, shall we?"

"Let's not," Alex said. "This is not a social call. We are here to try and broker peace."

"Humour me." Sebastian walked over and sat down, looking at them impatiently. Caspian remained standing, too, looking warily between all three of them. He'd lost weight, Avery thought, looking thinner than he had only weeks ago. His cheeks had hollowed out, and dark shadows were under his eyes. He looked ill.

Avery looked at Alex, trying to gauge what he was thinking, but he glanced at her and then at Sebastian, determined to maintain control. He strolled over to the window. "Quite the view you have, Faversham. Don't you think you have enough?"

"There's no such thing as enough." Sebastian leaned back, his legs crossed, his suit elegant, and his eyes watchful.

Alex turned around, and with the light behind him it was difficult to see his expression. "Why do want the grimoires?"

"None of your business," Sebastian shot back.

"Wrong. It *is* our business, because they're ours, gifted to us by our ancestors. And you've stolen one of them. Or should I say Caspian has, your lackey, running around doing your bidding?"

Caspian's eyes hardened, but he still glanced nervously at his father.

Sebastian continued, nonplussed. "Isn't Gil's death enough to convince you that we mean what we say?"

Avery stiffened. They had discussed this on the way over. Alicia had died last night, and it was likely that no one other than them knew what had happened.

"No," Alex said. "If anything, it's strengthened our resolve not to let you have the grimoires. You clearly have no respect for anything or anyone."

Sebastian rose to his feet swiftly and Avery felt the air in the room crackle with energy. It was as if Sebastian had unveiled his power, rather than drew it to him. "How dare you presume to know me!"

Alex stepped forward. "And how dare you presume to know *us*."

The energy in the room magnified as magical power flooded through them. Avery tensed, ready to attack, and she glanced at Caspian, who stood closest to her. He, of all of

136

them, seemed the calmest, but Avery knew how powerful he was, and how quickly he could unleash it.

Alex spoke again. "Why do you want the grimoires?"

Sebastian paused for a moment. "Because they contain something we need."

Alex leaned against Sebastian's desk, arms crossed in front of him. "What if we keep the grimoires, and you tell us what you need, and we'll share that—if we feel it won't harm us. Then we both have what we want."

"Because it is not in our interest to let you keep them."

"It is not in our interest to let you have them, either. Surely," Alex persisted, "we must be able to come to some sort of compromise. Our families have been fighting for generations. Yours engineered Helena's death at the hands of the Witchfinder General, and manipulated others to support you. Haven't you done enough?" Alex was getting angry now, his voice rising with his indignation. "These grimoires are years old. We have no interest in warring with you, or using our new abilities and powers to attack you. We just want to live peacefully alongside you. Two magical communities, co-existing together."

Sebastian laughed, his head thrown back. "You're a fool. You have no idea what those grimoires can do."

"We know there's a hidden spell at the back of them. A spell that bound Octavia. Is that it? Is that what you want? To release her?"

Avery thought she detected a snort from Caspian, but when she glanced at him, he stood impassive, watching his father. He turned to her, aware of her gaze. His eyes swept across her, a look of curiosity and doubt, and Avery had the feeling that they were missing a key piece of information.

Sebastian answered, a carefully schooled response. "Octavia's soul should be released. But we will do that, and we need your grimoires."

"No, you need the spell. Not the grimoires. We'll do it for you, or copy the spell for you. As long as the demon is not released."

Sebastian thought for a moment. "No, that's unacceptable. But a kind offer," he said, sarcastically.

Now Avery *knew* they were missing something. They had just made a perfectly good offer, and it had been rejected for no good reason. It seemed Alex thought so, too.

"You're hiding something, Sebastian. We'll find out what. And then you'll wish you had accepted our offer." Alex looked at Avery and stood, ready to leave, "At least we tried."

Sebastian laughed again. "We have one grimoire, and we *will* get the rest. I believe you have only one left to find?" He glanced at Avery, and she felt the full power in his gaze pierce her core.

They didn't answer, and he laughed some more. "We'll know when you have it, and then we'll take them all. Taking the Jackson's was merely a demonstration of our power. Believe me when I say it will be better to hand them over. Surely, one death is enough?" he said, revealing he had no idea about Alicia.

"Ah, about that," Alex said, stepping closer until he was now only a few paces from Sebastian. "Unfortunately, there was a small incident last night. Alicia, your mole, was killed by her own demons, with a little help from us. So, we're sort of even on the death stakes."

"You're a liar," Sebastian accused, his eyes narrowing. He glanced at Caspian, whose look of doubt rattled Sebastian even more.

"I wouldn't lie about something so serious, Seb. Try and call her. Now. Go on, I can wait."

Sebastian looked as if he was wrestling with obeying Alex's suggestion, but curiosity finally got the better of him and he pulled his phone from his pocket and punched in a number.

They stood waiting silently while Alex moved closer to Avery. When it was clear that no one was answering, he phoned another number. "Put me through to Alicia," he said abruptly. He listened, watching Alex and Avery with hostility. "What do you mean, she's not in?" He paused. "Keep trying, and call me."

He rang off and stared at them for a moment, and then threw his phone at Alex.

Avery was about to laugh, it seemed so unexpectedly juvenile, but in a split second the phone changed into what looked like a dragon, the size of a large bird of prey that screeched as it rushed at Alex, its wings outstretched, cruel talons curving with malice, and flames pouring from its gaping mouth.

Alex rolled and simultaneously threw out a rope of pure energy, lashing at the creature and throwing it back in a high arc across the room and to the window.

At the same time, Avery blocked an attack from Caspian and Sebastian, as they both threw a stream of fire at her. She responded with a jet of super-heated air, knocking Caspian off his feet and into the corridor, where he crashed against the wall. However, Sebastian remained standing, his pupils all black with no hint of white. Avery felt her breath catch. *What was happening?*

He grew taller and broader, and for the first time Avery was aware of how much power he wielded. It was terrifying.

He reached out his arm, and although he was halfway across the room, she felt her breath catch as her chest tightened.

Alex, however, had not finished, and as she struggled to repel Sebastian's magic, Alex jumped to his feet. The dragon wheeled and attacked him again, soaring across the room. Alex shattered the huge window at the back of the room and threw the dragon out of it with a well-placed blast of energy.

The sound was deafening. Glass exploded everywhere, and the dragon screeched as it rolled over and over in the air, now outside the building and high above the street.

Sebastian's concentration broke immediately, and Avery was able to breathe again.

For a brief second Avery watched him as he tried to regain control of the dragon, which now out in the open, also seemed to be swelling in size. A dragon was in Harecombe. A real, live dragon.

Alex grabbed her hand and pulled her towards the window. "Jump."

"Are you insane?" The words were barely out of her mouth when he kicked the jagged edges of glass away and dragged her through the window; they dropped like stones.

And then suddenly they weren't falling anymore, but floating, and she had the presence of mind to throw a veil of shadow over them as they streamed down the side of the building and landed at the corner.

It was chaos on the street. Glass was lying on the ground, some people were screaming, cars had screeched to a halt, and horns were blaring at those who were standing in the middle of the road, staring at the creature that now perched on the shattered window, five floors up. No one was looking at them.

They ran across the street to Alex's car, jumped in, and raced away, threading through the chaos with barely a backward glance.

15

Risking being pulled for speeding, Alex kept his foot down until they were well out of Harecombe. He finally stopped at a large country pub, the car park packed with customers, and they grabbed an outside table and a pint.

They both took a long drink of beer while Avery tried to still her jumbled thoughts. Their conversation in the car had been stilted and mostly consisted of, *"Are we being followed?"* *"No, not yet. Keep going."*

Now sitting in the pub, surrounded by others, she said, "I can't believe you dragged me out of a window. I thought you were trying to kill me."

He laughed. "Idiot. I'm not suicidal."

"I wish you'd have warned me."

"Yes, like I had time for that. While I was battling a *dragon!*"

She stared at him for a second and then burst out laughing, and he laughed, too, until they were both giggling hysterically. Other people turned to stare, and that made Avery worse. "Holy crap," she said, trying to control herself, "It really was, wasn't it? I mean, I wasn't hallucinating. It was a dragon!"

"Bloody Hell, Ave, what have we got ourselves into?" Alex looked like an excited kid who'd just learned he was going to Hogwarts.

"Why are we even laughing? I mean, it's not funny," Avery said, still laughing. "Sebastian's a psychopath, and he conjures dragons. Out of a bloody phone!"

"That was priceless. The look on his face!"

"I think I'm hysterical. This is not a normal reaction to being attacked by a dragon and jumping out of a fifth floor window. Oh, and nearly being crushed by a Darth Vader move."

"Yeah, it was a bit Vader-y." Alex sipped his pint, having finally stopped laughing. "So what's he hiding?"

"I don't know, but I don't think he gives a crap about Octavia's trapped soul. We're missing something. Something big. Something that I think will benefit us, and he's terrified of us getting—and it's not just the grimoires."

Alex fell silent, thinking. "Your grimoire contains the first spell. It *must* tell us more about what it really does. We have to find it." He downed his pint. "Come on, let's go back to yours and get searching."

***

When they arrived back at Happenstance Books, they entered through the main shop and found Sally stocking shelves, while Dan served an old couple struggling beneath a pile of books.

Sally looked across at them and smirked. "You two look like you've been up to no good. You haven't been to Harecombe, have you?"

"Why?" Avery asked nervously.

Alex headed to the rear door and said, "I'll head up and put the kettle on."

"No, no, no," Sally said. "Not until you've seen this."

She nodded to Dan and headed to the back room where she pulled her phone out of her pocket. "It's all over social media and the news. Some guy filmed this." She showed them a short clip of the corner of the harbour in Harecombe where Kernow Shipping stood. The filming was jerky, but they saw cars screeching to a halt, horns blaring, glass on the pavement and road, and people staring and pointing. When the camera swung upwards, you could see a shattered window and a flash of something dark, but nothing else.

Avery glanced at Alex, relieved. *No dragon. How would the Favershams have explained that? How did they get rid of it?* Sebastian must have acted quickly to get it under control.

"There were reports of a strange creature crashing out of the window, but all the company said was that a display from a local carnival had broken a window."

"Well, there you go. What's that got to do with us?" Avery said, wide-eyed.

Sally looked between the two of them, clearly not believing any of it. "So, I suppose you won't be helping in the shop this afternoon?" she asked Avery.

"Not for a couple of hours, but I can relieve you for lunch," she said, checking her watch and finding it was already after one in the afternoon. No wonder her stomach was rumbling. "Sorry, it is lunch."

Sally waved her off, "No, we're fine, carry on. I'll shout if I need you, though."

"Cheers, Sally," Avery said, giving her a hug before following Alex upstairs.

"Bloody hell, I'm starving!" Alex declared, weaving through Avery's messy flat to the kitchen. He looked around, bemused, as he stepped over books and magazines, and paused to fuss over the cats as they wound around his ankles, almost tripping him up. "Have you got any food in the fridge?"

"Of course! It's just cleaning I'm not very good at," she said sheepishly. She switched on the TV and found the local lunchtime news. While Alex foraged through the fridge, she started to tidy, keeping an eye on the newscast. The headline item was the shattered glass window at Harecombe, but other than the short video, all it suggested was that the window had been accidentally broken, and no one was hurt. A representative from the business, who Avery didn't recognise, reassured the news team that it was purely accidental. Avery snorted. Their actions would have only increased tensions between them, but at least they had tried.

Just as the news item finished, her phone rang, and she looked at the caller and groaned. "Hi Newton," she said with a raised voice, attracting Alex's attention. He looked around and mouthed, *Oops.*

"What the bloody hell have you been doing?" Newton raged from the phone.

"Whatever do you mean?" she asked, feigning ignorance.

"You know exactly what I bloody mean. Briar *eventually* told me your plans, and we've just watched the news. What the hell have you done?"

"You're still at Briar's?" she asked, avoiding his question.

"Yes I bloody am, covered in demon burns. What have you done?"

She winced. "We went to discuss terms."

"Terms of bloody *what?*"

"Newton. Please stop swearing," she said, knowing it would infuriate him further. "We went to discuss the grimoire, let him know about Alicia, and then he set a dragon on us."

"A bloody *what?*"

"A dragon. A small one, the size of a bird of prey—which is actually quite large, as birds go. But not dragons. I believe they are normally bigger."

"Is this a joke?" he shouted.

"Unfortunately not. Sebastian Faversham is a mean bastard with a lot of power, and didn't like being told Alicia was dead. He made a dragon out of a phone. It was very impressive, if unexpected," she said, pacing across the room with nervous energy. "Alex fended it off and broke the window."

"You could have been bloody killed! Why didn't you ask me to come?"

"Unofficial witch business, you know that. You can't risk being involved, Newton."

He fell silent for a second. "You still should have told me."

"No, better you didn't know at all. Are you feeling okay this morning?"

He grunted. "A bit better. Briar knows her stuff."

"Yes, she does. Are you off sick?"

"Yes, I have no choice."

"Good. Stay there. Hopefully there'll be no repercussions. We kept your name out of things, but keep your head down for a few days. How's Briar?"

"She's fine. Hang on, she wants a word."

Avery heard shuffling as the phone was handed over, and then she heard Briar. "Avery, this is getting worse. Can't we stop this *thing* with the Faversfams?"

"We tried, Briar, he didn't want to listen. There's more going on than we realise."

"Were you and Alex hurt?" she asked, sounding worried.

"No. Please don't worry, just keep investigating your grimoire, and protect yourself. Keep Newton there for now, too."

As she hung up, she wondered how El and Reuben were, and while Alex was busy in the kitchen, Avery rang El. She answered quickly. "Hi, Avery."

"Hey, El. How are you two?"

"We're okay, just working through some stuff." She lowered her voice. "Reuben's really down. I've never seen him like this. I can't leave him."

"Have you managed to sort your shop out?"

"Yeah, Zoe's got it covered." Avery presumed Zoe was the immaculate guardian of the shop.

"Well, I've got news for you." She filled El in on their encounter and passed on the same advice she'd given to Briar; keep quiet for a few days and gather strength.

Avery didn't actually say what she really felt, which was that they'd entered a new stage of war with the Favershams. Although she and Alex had laughed about it at the pub, she had a feeling things were about to get a lot worse.

By the time she'd finished on the phone, Alex had finished cooking, and he brought in two plates, each loaded with a thick bacon and egg sandwich on crusty bread, and they headed upstairs to the attic room.

Avery had a large bite and sighed with pleasure. As she chewed, she rearranged some of the research on the wooden table, while Alex stood in front of the map, also chewing and thinking.

He pointed at the map. "What are the pins for?"

"I've marked the original houses of our families at the time of the hanging, but of course there's only Gil's and El's so far." She knew she should say 'Reuben's' now, but still couldn't get out of the habit.

"Now that we have the old records, the other addresses will be in there, won't they?" He turned to the table and rummaged through the trial transcripts.

Avery walked over to the map. "I have an address for Helena, but I think it was her mother's house that she lived in when she was young. She lived in a different one once she was married." She picked up a pin and marked the tiny cottage she had visited the other day.

Alex flicked through the book they had stolen from the Courtney Library. "The Ashworths, Briar's family, are listed as having lived on South Street. I wonder if that still exists?"

"It sounds familiar." Avery said, trying to find it on the map, before pulling her phone out of her pocket to Google it. As soon as the image popped up, she remembered it. "Yeah, it's at the top of the town, heading onto the moors. It's steep, if I remember correctly, and old, so it must be the same one."

"I wonder if the numbers are the same?" Alex mused. "It says number 51."

Avery punched the number in and watched the street view materialise. "Well, it's certainly 16th century. Decent size, too."

"Which is what you'd expect for a merchant." Alex marked it on the map with a red pin. "It's almost directly above El's Hawk House along the coast, and it's opposite to Helena's mother's."

"And diagonally opposite Gil's," Avery noticed.

Alex looked at her, puzzled. "Strangely symmetrical, don't you think?"

"Yes actually, but it must be a coincidence."

"Okay, I'm going to check my family's."

Alex turned his attention back to the book as Avery continued to study the map. She took another bite of her sandwich and then grunted as she remembered something else in Anne's papers. She rummaged through the pile on the table and pulled out an old map of White Haven. She pinned that up and noted the differences between the new and the old. The main shape of the town was the same, and the centre of the town was virtually unchanged, its tight network of streets straggling down to the harbour and along the beach, and inland up into the small valley which narrowed as it followed the curve of the hills down to the coast. The edges of the town were populated with new buildings, houses built in the 19th century.

Avery then picked up Samuel's book and flicked through it, finding a rough map of the town in the 16th century. It was far smaller, but the centre of the town still had the same shape. Layers on layers of history, Avery mused, and its secrets were lost in the foundations and the tide of humanity that had been born, lived, and died here. Until now.

Alex's exclamation disturbed her reverie. "Found it. Parsonage Road. Does that still exist?"

She Googled it quickly, and found it up higher in the centre of the town, close to the Parish Church of St Peters. "Of course, the old church at the top of the town," she said, pointing out the road on the map.

"It's almost dead centre between the Ashworth's place and Helena's," Alex said, marking it with another pin. He grabbed a pencil and drew a faint line between the four on the outside, and then stopped, puzzled. "No, that's not right—what would Parsonage Road link with?"

A thought struck Avery and she groaned, incredulous. "It couldn't be, could it?"

"What?" Alex asked, frowning at her.

She took the pencil from him, and drew a pentacle, linking all five buildings together. "What do you think?"

"Bloody hell. That works. And it aligns to the elements on the compass—each family's strength, each house marking the points. What's in the centre?" he asked, scrutinising the map.

Avery put her head next to his as they scanned the map. "The Church of All Souls. It's been there for centuries."

"The heart of the town, if not the true centre," Alex noted. It was too high to be the exact centre of town.

They both looked at each other, stunned. Avery elaborated. "The spirit of the town, locked within the centre of the pentacle. A place of power. Briar's spell—the grounding."

"A place where you would lock a spirit and a demon?"

"It has to be!" Avery exclaimed. "And where something else may be locked, too."

16

Alex paced the room while Avery again examined the map that appeared on the book they'd stolen from the Witch Museum. She lit a witch light, closed the blinds to block out the sunshine from the bright afternoon, and stared at the fine white markings that must be tantalisingly close.

"Come on, Alex, we need to be logical about possible hiding places for Helena's grimoire. We need an old building, something that's likely to have passages underneath, someplace accessible to her."

"Churches. There are four in White Haven. Old Haven Church where the Jackson's mausoleum is. And where there'll be a crypt. Then there's the Parish Church of St Peter's…"

"And the Church of All Souls in the centre of the pentagram," Avery said, finishing his sentence. "All will have crypts, all are old. The fourth is that Methodist church, but that's far too new."

"True. Then there are a lot of old, 16th century houses, but how likely are they to have tunnels beneath them?"

"And to have been accessible?" Avery added.

Alex continued to list buildings. "The old pubs along the harbour front and the centre of town. They have a big smuggling history, lots of tunnels there, probably."

"What if it's under Helena's family house, the point of Air on the pentagram?"

Alex rolled his eyes as the suggestions grew. "Where's the house she shared with her husband? It might be under there. In fact, the map may not be showing passages at all. It could even be a floor plan of a house, with the grimoire hidden in the walls."

"Or an attic."

"Elspeth's was hidden in the grounds of her house, Reuben's in the mausoleum—again, their property."

"But what about yours and Briar's? Who knows where they were originally hidden."

"There's the aquarium, that's an old building, recently converted, right by the sea wall."

"Or, of course, the Witch Museum."

"Or White Haven Museum?"

"I didn't even think of that." Avery said, annoyed with herself. It was another stone-built house that was on a street sitting along the harbour, with a commanding view over the sea. It had been gifted to the town by the family who owned it, and was now owned by the National Trust.

"But, what link would Helena have to it?" Alex pointed out.

"Excellent, very logical. Let's rule that out."

Alex was already looking for Helena's second address. "Penny Lane, that was Helena's house with her husband," he said, looking up. "That must be the one leading off the high street."

"It is. It's a lovely old street actually," Avery said, remembering its mellow stone and half-timbered buildings.

"Let's try to imagine Helena's thoughts. The five witches—or witch families—have just performed a big spell, one that mustn't be undone, the Witchfinder's coming, and you need to hide your book. Where would you go?"

"I would avoid my house, it would feel too obvious. I'd also probably avoid my mother's house, too," she said, thinking of the tiny cottage she'd stopped in front of the other day. She searched through the papers on the table and consulted her family tree to check dates. "Helena's mother had already died by then anyway, that's why I didn't see her name in the trials—at least she was spared that horror."

Alex frowned. "We're missing something."

Avery smacked her head with her palm. "We're forgetting the Newtons! Is it worth finding where he lived?"

Alex shrugged, "We can, but why would she hide it with the Justice of the Peace?"

"I would have thought it's the perfect place to hide it. Who would think to look there?"

"Fair enough, that does have a certain logic." He consulted the letters that had been sent to Newton by Thaddeus Faversham, scanning them quickly. "Also Penny Lane! Next door to Helena's!" He looked up at her, his pupils large in the muted light. "They were neighbours—he'd have known her well."

"No wonder he felt so annoyed when he couldn't save her. Do you think he knew she really was a witch? But knew she was trustworthy, too?"

"Maybe," he shrugged, unconvinced. "They may have had cellars that could be linked. He would never have known what she had concealed. It's worth checking. Those buildings are shops now, right?"

Avery consulted Google Maps again and then laughed. "Of course they are! I'm so stupid."

"What?"

"Both Helena's house and Newton's are now one building." She looked at him expectantly, as if he should know.

"So? What building? A big shop?"

"It's a restaurant, quite a flash one—Penny Lane Bistro."

Alex grinned. "Public access! Great! What you up to this evening?"

"What I'm up to every evening—looking for this bloody grimoire."

"May I take you out for dinner?"

Avery laughed. "Really? You don't want to sneak in after they're closed?"

"Of course I want to sneak in after they're closed, but we can check it out officially first."

"It's expensive!"

"So?" He frowned, crossed his arms, and leaned back against the table. "You don't want to be seen in public with me?"

Avery huffed at Alex's annoyed expression. *Was he serious?* "I'm seen with you all the time! Are you crazy?"

"As friends. This is a date."

"A date—like a proper, wine-and-dine date?"

"So you'll sleep with me, but not go out to dinner with me?"

Now she knew he had to be winding her up. "I had a pint with you today! Besides, I wasn't sure how serious the whole sleeping together thing was."

His face darkened, and she realised she had made a serious error. "So you're back to thinking I'm just a womaniser? And you're what, the female equivalent? I'm just a quick roll between the sheets for you? You know what? Maybe I should go."

He put the book down, and turned.

"No! Alex, please—I'm sorry!" Panic flooded her at the thought that she'd ruined a perfectly great, if uncertain relationship. "You know what, we're both to blame—we sleep together, and then that's it! I don't know what to think *this* is!" She softened her voice. "You are not *just a quick roll in between the sheets*. You're more than that. And, I know you're not a womaniser. I'm sorry, sometimes I feel a little insecure. You're very..." she hesitated.

He turned back to her and leaned back on the table again, his eyes narrowed. "Unreliable, arrogant, annoying?" He quoted all the things she'd said before.

"Hot. Very, very hot. And clever and quick-witted. And I wonder why you're interested in me," she said in a rush, fearing she'd lose her nerve if she didn't say what she really thought right now. "This past few weeks has been great, but I didn't want to presume too much."

His shoulders dropped and she felt his anger ebb slightly. "Have you noticed how hot *you* are lately? And brave, and funny, and powerful?"

She flushed. "Alex, don't tease. I'm not those things."

He reached forward and brushed her hair from her face, his hands sending a tingle all down her spine. "I think you're very beautiful, Avery, and I can't stop thinking about you. And, as well as being gorgeous, you're a kick-ass witch who I trust implicitly. And trust me when I say that I haven't had as much fun with anyone for a long time as I had with you today. Now, would you like to go to dinner with me tonight?"

She held her hand over his, pressing it against her cheek. "Yes. I would love to."

"Good. I'll meet you here at seven-fifteen." He kissed her softly and then left, a hum of residual energy left in the space.

Holy shit. What had just happened? Her heart was racing, and she paced the room nervously, the cats watching her through their narrowed eyes as they half-dozed on the sofa. *Breathe, Avery, breathe.* He hadn't declared his love, he'd just told her she was beautiful, and gorgeous, and brave, and powerful. And he'd looked at her in a way he hadn't before, even when they were having sex.

What the hell was she going to wear?

***

By the time Alex arrived at 7:15 Avery had wasted hours, unable to concentrate on any of Anne's paperwork, or Helena's map.

She had eventually given up and showered, and then tried on and discarded half a dozen dresses and shoes before sternly reminding herself that she knew Alex, had slept with him, and didn't need to panic. She finally settled on a black, knee-length dress and three-inch tan wedges, which showed off her legs. It seemed with this simple request for a date that everything had changed, had become more serious. Official. But of course, it hadn't. She was imagining things.

When Alex turned up, she couldn't help but gasp. "Wow, you look good."

"So do you," he said, kissing her cheek.

He wore black boots, dark jeans, a black V-neck shirt, and a dark suit jacket. His hair was tied in a man-bun. It was still Alex, not too groomed, but just groomed enough—he still had dark stubble and his usual grin on his face.

He took her hand. "Ready?"

"Ready," she agreed, grabbing her leather bag.

Avery couldn't help but smile as they strolled down the street, but for once they both seemed a little awkward. They ended up both speaking at the same time, and they laughed. "Ladies first," Alex said.

"I've brought the plans with me, just in case."

"You're not planning on having a witch light floating over our table, are you?

"No! Are we planning on breaking in tonight?"

"I think we should, if it looks likely." He squeezed her hand, "Maybe not in those shoes, though?"

"Oh ye of little faith," she laughed, echoing his line from earlier that day.

Penny Lane, as Avery had remembered, was a narrow, cobbled street lined with 16th century buildings, made of stone and timber. The stone was a warm amber colour, quarried locally, while the wood not only framed the windows but covered some of the upper walls, and were painted in soft whites and muted yellows and pinks.

Most of the buildings were now shops, the lower floors for retail, the upper floors either storerooms or flats. Some buildings were Bed and Breakfasts, and were very popular with tourists. Hanging baskets filled with a profusion of summer bedding plants were hung all down the street, as they were all over the town.

The bistro's entrance was a discreet wooden door, set back under a deep porch. Mullioned windows on either side of the door, with candles glittering on the sills, provided a glimpse into the interior. Once inside, a small counter had been set up by the entrance to receive guests. The inner walls had been knocked out, and it was now a large, open space, broken up only by columns and archways. The ceiling was still timbered, and the whole place was an artful blend of old and new.

Across the room was a long wall of paned glass revealing a courtyard garden, and she heard the clink of glasses and murmured conversation drifting across the room.

Avery breathed deeply with pleasure as she gazed at the white linen tablecloths, soft lighting, glasses, and silverware.

Their table was in the corner, overlooking the courtyard, and as they sat, Avery noticed that many other tables were already filling up. "We were lucky to get a table here."

"Perks of being in the trade—I sort of know the manager."

"Do you think he'd let us in the cellars as a sort of favour?"

"I don't know him that well," he said, looking at the wine menu.

She sighed. "I'm trying to avoid breaking in again. It's becoming a habit."

"Fun, though," he mused, glancing up at her with a smirk.

"I don't think Newton would think so."

"He's got Briar to distract him. And besides, I don't think it will be as bad as attacking Faversham Central."

Avery looked at the menu, finding it difficult to concentrate. Their friends were split into two camps, possibly vulnerable to attack. Briar was on her own, magically speaking, and so was El. Avery wasn't sure how effective Reuben would be right now. The more she thought about this morning, the more rash she felt they'd been. And here they were, having a meal in the gorgeous Penny Lane Bistro. She looked up at Alex, his head bent over the menu, and her heart tightened. *What if he got hurt?*

Alex looked up, startling her out of her thoughts. "Stop worrying and tell me what wine you'd like."

"Sorry. We're all split up tonight. I was just thinking how vulnerable we are."

"All the more reason to find your grimoire, find out what the spell really is, and get more bargaining power."

She nodded. "You're right. A very large Tempranillo, please."

"And this is a date, remember. People will think I'm a crap date if you don't cheer up."

She laughed, "Sorry, this is great, thank you. I haven't been anywhere like this for a long time."

"Me neither." He looked around. "Have you noticed? No cameras in here."

"I should think not. They're hardly conducive to romance and fine dining. I bet there's some out back, though," she said, nodding towards the courtyard.

They were interrupted by the waiter, and once they'd ordered, Avery said, "It's weird, isn't it? This is where Helena once lived. She walked through these rooms, slept here, ate here. Her children were born here. And she'd have been arrested here." She felt a rush of emotion and stopped for a moment, trying to calm her thoughts.

"And now we'll get revenge for her," Alex said. "Somewhere in these walls could be her legacy to you."

She nodded. "There are a couple of doors to restricted staff areas—do you think there's still access to cellars?"

"This is a restaurant now. I bet they use it for storing wine. In fact," Alex said, staring outside, "I can see a large hatch set into the floor. Must be an outside entrance."

Avery followed his gaze and saw a dark rectangle in the courtyard, butting up against the wall of the building. "I see it. Perfect!"

"How agile are you in those shoes?"

"Extremely. Why?"

"Wandering around White Haven in combat gear at night, in the centre of town, will be very suspicious. When we've finished here, we'll head to the pub and then come back after closing. Sound good?"

"Great."

"Excellent, and now we can enjoy our date," he said, teasing her, and making her feel self-conscious all over again.

***

After the meal, Alex and Avery headed to a small pub called The Startled Hare a few doors down from the bistro, and stayed there until closing.

They tried not to talk about the missing grimoires, the Favershams, or magic, and instead talked about anything and everything else. Avery wasn't sure if the meal was a good idea or not, as she now knew that she was pretty much head over heels with Alex. And they had so much fun together. She felt she was like a schoolgirl again, and every now and then she'd find him looking at her speculatively, which made her heart race even faster.

They were nearly the only people left on the street as the bar staff ushered them outside after last orders. They strolled past the bistro, and seeing it was now empty, other than a couple of waiters doing a final clear up, they walked up and away from the town, and then tried to find the alley that ran behind the bistro. The cool night breeze caressed her skin, and Avery pulled her lightweight cardigan close. Alex pulled her into him, wrapping his arms around her as they tried to look as inconspicuous as possible.

Towards the end of Penny Lane they paused outside an alley that disappeared around the back of the buildings.

"This way," Alex said, checking down the street and then pulling Avery after him.

They passed wheelie bins full of rubbish outside the side entrances of the shops on either side, and then turned left heading down towards the bistro. The fences were high at the back of the shops, and most places were quiet as it was long past their closing. They passed the pub and then paused as they saw a gate open and close further down. A waiter emerged from the shadows to put some rubbish into a bin, and then disappeared back behind the fence.

"That must be it," Alex said, and they moved closer, peering through the wooden planks.

"How long until they go?" Avery asked.

"Can't be long now."

They wrapped themselves in a shadow spell, waited another fifteen minutes after the lights went out, and then they eased the gate open with another spell and edged into the courtyard.

Two cameras were high on the wall, one angled towards the glass doors leading into the restaurant, and the other towards the cellar door, and there was a security light. Avery immobilised them all with a whisper, and after checking that the restaurant was in complete darkness, they unlocked the cellar door in the floor and headed down the steps into darkness, pulling the door shut above them.

They stood listening for a few moments, but there was only silence.

Avery conjured a witch light, and its cool, white light showed a paved stone floor, and racks of wine and other stores stretching away into darkness. She pulled the book with the map from her bag and studied it.

The map was long and narrow, much like the cellar space. "This could be it," she whispered, showing Alex.

"Well, there's not much cellar to our left. We're at the edge of the building, but it should go all the way down there," he said, pointing under the main restaurant area.

The cellars, unlike the restaurant above, were still made up of small rooms, all interconnected by archways. The map showed similar-sized blocks, and a tiny pentagram was marked on an interior wall.

"Come on, let's get our bearings," Alex said, leading the way.

They snaked around the free standing shelving housing wine bottles and other supplies, heading into the centre of the cellar. A steep staircase rose to a door set into the wall, but they passed it for now, checking what else was down there. They came to a thick wall, which looked as if it marked where the two buildings would have been divided, and walking through the archway in it, passed another set of stairs which had been bricked up at the top.

The stores ended, and the rest of the rooms were empty, other than a few old boxes, chairs, and endless dust. Avery suppressed the urge to sneeze.

"Which house was which?" Alex asked.

"The one that's now the main dining area was Helena's, the kitchen area is Newton's."

"So we're under Helena's now. Where's that pentagram marked?"

"It's hard to say, I'm not sure which way up the map should be. It looks to be on an inner wall of the first or last room, depending on how it's placed."

"Let's check here then first, just in case."

They headed to the old stone wall and examined it carefully. The stone work was rough and almost a foot thick, but looked intact. Even with the witch light floating above them, nothing was marked or looked suspicious. Then they tried the surrounding walls for good measure, before heading back to the side of the building where they'd entered.

They headed to the far wall, and worked their way back.

"It should be here," Avery said, confused. "If this is the right place. See, the second wall in has the pentagram mark, but there's no wall."

"But there is," Alex said, pointing upwards. Above them was a couple of feet of wall spanning a third of the cellar and forming an archway, separating one section from another. "It's just a very small wall."

Avery pulled a torch from her bag and pointed it at the stones above them. "They're so tightly fitted together, but I think I can see an edge sticking out."

"We need a closer look." He looked around searching for a ladder, but there was nothing in sight. "There's no way I can reach that, it's a least nine feet up."

"But I can, if you boost me." Avery decided there was no way she was leaving without checking this out.

Alex crouched down. "All right. Get on my shoulders. And keep your voice down, just in case."

Avery juggled the torch as she got into position, and Alex rose to his feet slowly.

"Shit," Avery said, as she wobbled and grabbed the wall to steady herself.

When she was in position, she shone her torch onto the spot. Close up there was definitely a seam. "Alex, I'm right," she whispered.

"Well, get on with it," he hissed back, and shone his torch up towards the wall.

For a few seconds Avery worked at the bricks, trying to pull them loose and failing miserably. When Alex shifted position, she wobbled and leaned heavily on one of the surrounding bricks, and with a distinct click, the entire section popped forward. Her heart was now pounding in her chest. She wiggled the bricks free until half a dozen in an uneven rectangle eased into her hands.

"Alex, hold this," she said, passing them down.

For a few seconds they juggled torches and bricks, and then with both hands free, Avery turned her own torch into the hole. It was a small, dry space hollowed out of the wall, and something was in there. She pulled out a thick, heavy object the size of a large book wrapped in oilskin and put her torch in the gap left behind.

"I think we've found it," she whispered. She carefully opened up the oilskin, and beneath it was a leather-bound book.

"Well?" Alex asked, adjusting his position and making Avery wobble again.

Triumph and relief filled her voice. "Yes! It's Helena's book. The sign for air is on the cover."

"Excellent, let's get those bricks back in place and get out of here."

17

Alex deposited Avery at her door with a kiss that left her tingling right down to her toes.

"You're not coming in?"

"I better put in a full day at work tomorrow. And besides, I think you deserve some time to examine the book. I'll see you tomorrow, though?"

"Yes. And thanks for tonight. I really enjoyed it."

"Me, too. Stay safe." And then he disappeared, leaving her with an ache that she wasn't sure the book was going to fill.

After making herself a chamomile and lavender tea, she headed to bed and curled up with the book on her lap, a cat on either side. She could barely believe it. After days of searching, she finally had it. Thank the gods it hadn't been put in one of those crazy rune boxes.

The leather creaked under Avery's fingers as she eased it open and she felt a tingle of magic run through her.

Like the other grimoires, a long list of names filled the front pages of all the witches that had gone before her, and Helena's was the last. She stroked the page, feeling the worn paper, soft beneath her fingers, and suddenly, the awareness of a presence nearby. She looked up, as did the cats, rousing from their slumber as they looked wide-eyed at the door. The room remained empty, but a soft breeze fluttered around her carrying the scent of violets, and she felt a breath on her cheek and the sensation of a kiss, and then it was gone.

Helena.

Avery's hand flew to her cheek and tears filled her eyes as an aching loneliness and sorrow swept through her—and then something else. Relief.

She called out, "Helena, don't go. Talk to me."

But Helena had gone, leaving her blessing, or so it felt to Avery.

She wiped away a tear and turned back to the book. She took her time, turning the pages carefully, trying to decipher the spidery writing. A witch light hovered at her shoulder, and she could see runes and symbols marked on the pages. Unable to contain her curiosity, she headed to the end of the grimoire and found the hidden spell. It began: *The First Part: To Gather the Four Points and Bind them to the Task.*

But then, rather than the spell, there was a note written by Helena.

> *"It is with great trepidation and sorrow that we make this spell. We have lived in White Haven for years, healing, making charms, protecting the poor and rich alike. We seek to do no harm, only good, and we have promised ourselves that we will not bend from our task. And yet, circumstances have made us change our decision.*
>
> *"And it is my fault. So here I make my confession, for it is because of me that this spell has come to pass. Before I met my husband, when I was young and foolish, I lay with Thaddeus Faversham, and before long found that I bore his child. He promised me everything, but in the end, gave me nothing. I could have got rid of the child, it is in my power to do so, but I could not, and so to conceal my shame, I married my husband, cast a spell to delay the birth, and then lied to say it was not full term. And he knew nothing.*

"My daughter, Ava, is now eight, and is a great joy, and a sweet sister to Louisa. But recently my dear husband Edward died, and Octavia Faversham has decided that Ava must live with them now. She and Thaddeus have finally acknowledged (privately) that she is a Faversham, and is arrogant enough to believe that I do not deserve to raise my own daughter. Ava already shows signs of power well before one would expect it, and I believe it is her power rather than blood that motivates Octavia. And Octavia is powerful enough to steal her, too, and nobody would know or remember.

"I will not countenance it. I am furious, and have devised a plan to silence her forever. She will never rest until she has what is mine, and neither will Thaddeus. They think I am alone and vulnerable without my husband, but they are wrong. My power has never been stronger, and the other four families will stand with me. We will banish Octavia forever, locked within the earth with her pet demon she threatens to unleash. Thaddeus will think twice before he threatens me again.

"But it shall come at a cost. With great spells come real sacrifice, and I am sacrificing my power to keep my daughter. It will weaken all of us, and it may be that the others will live to regret it. But they are also now being threatened by the Favershams, and so they must do this to protect themselves, too. A life without magic— or very little, at least—will be like a life half-lived. It may well be that it takes my daughter's power, too.

"It is my intention to break this spell, when the time is right. I have no idea when that will be, but if not in my lifetime, maybe by the hand and tongue of some ancestor I shall never know. I have therefore written the spell that will bind Octavia, and also the spell to break it, and the exact orders of these incantations are described below. This grimoire is the key to all.

"The spell has been split into five parts, and all five witches must be present to cast it, and all five to break it. It encompasses White Haven itself, bound within the very earth of the town, cast in the heart of it. My part is written here, the other parts are hidden in the other grimoires.

"I have no idea of the repercussions it may cause. It may be that this spell echoes through the years, and I would beg forgiveness of anyone who reads this.

"But a warning to those who choose to break it—the power that is bound within the spell will be unleashed. If you are my descendant, your powers will grow, and your rightful inheritance will be replenished. And I encourage you to do so. You will claim your place within the world, as will all the other witches who stand with you.

"I wish you luck, for once the spell is broken, Octavia will also return. Beware her demon."

Below the note was the spell, complex and layered, with half a dozen ingredients, and then below that, a final word.

"It is done, and I am left weaker than I ever imagined. I fear I have cursed White Haven forever, and our enmity with the Faversbams will be sealed down the years. And now I hear the Witchfinder comes, and I must hide the grimoire forever.

Forgive me,
Helena"

Avery felt tears pricking her eyes again. *Poor Helena.* To have had a child with Thaddeus, and for him to abandon her was awful in itself, especially at that time, but to then threaten to take her was even worse. No wonder Helena had chosen to perform the spell. No wonder either that she could not fight back when she had been accused by the Witchfinder— Thaddeus would have known her powers were almost gone. He must have hated her to condemn her to such a death.

And Avery's true powers—hers and Helena's, now one in the same—were bound beneath White Haven, as were Alex's, El's, Reuben's and Briar's. Did this mean that the powers they had now were a fraction of what they could have? Did it still apply? Or had their powers eventually returned over the centuries?

Avery flopped back on the pillow, her head spinning. Helena said the powers would be *unleashed*. What did *that* mean? Would they flood through them like a tidal wave— would it flood the town? Or was all this just a fairy tale? A tale of long ago that had no power over them now, other than with words?

But then she thought of the Favershams. Why would they attack with demons if they didn't think the threat was real? She laughed. No wonder Sebastian had gone along with their conversation the other day. He didn't give a crap about Octavia's soul. He just didn't want them to get their powers back. Why, though? It wasn't as if they would attack the Favershams. They could co-exist as much as they had for years.

So many questions. Avery needed to speak to the others. One thing was certain, however. She knew she wanted to release their powers, regardless of crazy Octavia and her demon. It was their birthright, and she wanted it back. And that meant getting Reuben's grimoire back, as well.

Avery pulled the book to her chest and settled in for the night. She was going to study this book from cover to cover, in case there were more hidden secrets yet to be revealed.

18

Avery entered the shop with gritty eyes and a head full of questions. Sally took one look at her and plonked a coffee down in front of her.

"Here you go. Another late night?"

Avery nodded, sipping the hot drink with relish. "Yes, just catching up on some reading."

Sally smirked. "Really? Because I saw you heading into *The Startled Hare* last night, with Alex."

Avery met her eyes slowly. "We had a meal and went to the pub. And then I went home—*alone*."

"So it's official, then? Rather than this, 'oh, we're just friends doing some research...'" Sally said, adopting a sing-song voice.

"We're seeing how things go," Avery said, itching to spell Sally into silence, but feeling that would be way too mean.

A grin split Sally's face. "Excellent. I've always liked Alex. He's good for you."

Avery spluttered. "Don't be ridiculous. I'm going to open the shop."

Avery took her coffee with her, feeling her cheeks growing hot even as she walked away. She lit a few incense sticks on her way through the shop, and reinforced the spell that helped customers find the book they never knew they wanted.

All day she felt her mind was barely on the job, and she went through the motions as if she was in a trance, pacing out the day until she went to Alex's. He'd texted mid-morning to say he'd invited the others over that evening, and that they'd all accepted. She hoped Newton had some idea of how they were going to get the Jackson grimoire back.

By late afternoon, Avery was tidying the shelves in the far corner of the shop, which housed the esoteric section, when she felt something behind her. She swung around, alarmed, and found Caspian Faversham blocking her from the rest of the shop. His face was white and pinched, and he looked even worse than he had yesterday when they had attacked Kernow Shipping.

"Get out of my shop," she hissed, her hands balling with energy.

"I'm here to talk."

"You cannot possibly have anything to say that I'd want to hear."

"My father suggests a deal."

She was about to push past him, when she stopped and looked at him suspiciously. "What deal?"

"Hand over the grimoires, and no one else dies."

"You can stick your threats up your arse, Caspian. And you can tell your self-righteous wanker of a father to do the same. They're *our* books. Do you think we'd let Gil die in vain? You *murderer*," she spat at him.

She could feel wind whipping up around her, and the chimes hanging in the window alcove started to tinkle. She tried to subdue her annoyance, not wanting to attract attention.

Caspian's dark eyes felt as if they could pin her to the wall. "I didn't mean to kill Gil."

"Liar! I presume you didn't try to kill Reuben, either, at Old Haven Church. Your powers got away from you, did they? And Alicia wasn't trying to kill Reuben when she summoned demons in his own house? And what about the two people killed by the demons here in White Haven? Innocent people. Oh, that's right, you said normal people didn't count," she recounted, remembering their conversation on the beach.

"We started badly, I admit. We suggest a truce," he said, remaining solidly in her way.

She took a step back. "What's going on? Why would you suggest a truce now? Your father set a dragon on us for suggesting this very thing!"

"You shocked him about Alicia. We now believe you, and he wishes to compromise."

Something felt very wrong. She tried to see over his shoulder. *Sally*. She was 'innocent people.' "Where's Sally?"

A slow smile crept up Caspian's face. "She'll be fine. So long as you give us the grimoires."

White-hot anger spread through her, as did ice-cold fear. "Don't you dare hurt her, or I swear, I will kill you."

"You're not the one in the position of power here are you, Avery?"

"Neither are you, without those grimoires. You see, I now know why you want them, and it has nothing to do with poor old Octavia's trapped soul."

Caspian's eyes flashed with a hint of doubt.

She continued, "It's about the increased power we'll have when we unleash the binding spell. And believe me, we'll do it."

Caspian's menace increased as he stepped towards her and she felt his power pressing on her like a wall. "Not without Reuben's grimoire, you won't. And you will *never* find it. Five spells, five witches. You can't possibly do it without that portion. Give it up now, and let Sally come home. She has two children, doesn't she? It would be a shame to see them grow up motherless."

Avery knew he was goading her, and she wanted to let her power fly, to rip off his face and shred his smile to pieces. But then she smelled violets on the air again and felt a presence close to her, filling her with warmth and strength. *Helena.* And then she suddenly knew how they could break the spell.

She took a deep breath and stepped back from Caspian, careful not to give anything away. He must think she was scared and powerless, so she dropped her shoulders and looked defeated. "I need to speak to the others."

"Do it quickly—you're running out of time."

He couldn't possibly know she had found Helena's book. She needed to lie, really well. Witches were good at detecting lies. "But I haven't found Helena's book yet. We can't deliver them."

"But you have a map," he said, slightly annoyed.

"And zero clue as to what it's a map of!"

"Well, you had better work quickly. You have until midnight to deliver them to my father's home."

"It's not long enough—I've been looking for weeks," she said, panic-stricken. "And what do I tell Sally's husband?"

"That's your problem." Caspian's smug smile of superiority returned. "I look forward to seeing you later."

He turned, walked around the corner of the shelving, and disappeared.

Avery raced across the shop, hoping he'd merely been frightening her. "Sally? Sally!"

One of the locals, an elderly man with grey hair, turned and answered. "She headed to the back, love, with a young lady."

Avery now felt sick with fear. They really had taken her. She ran through the door into the back of the shop and found Sally's hex bag on the floor, the contents scattered.

Sally was gone.

***

"They've taken Sally? Your employee?" Newton was seething. "That's kidnapping. I'll arrest every single one of them."

"She's my *friend*. And you know you can't," Avery reasoned, biting back her annoyance. "We have to break the binding spell. That's our only hope. Then we'll have the power to fight the Favershams and rescue Sally. *And* get the grimoire back. And we only have until midnight to do it."

"Midnight! *Tonight?*" Alex exclaimed, his eyes wide.

"Yes. I'm sorry," Avery said, looking at all of them.

She stood in the centre of Alex's flat, dressed for battle. She was wearing her black skinny jeans, a fitted tee, low-heeled ankle boots, and her slim fitting leather jacket.

The lights were low and the mood was grim. Reuben was still distraught about Alicia and Gil's death; his mood had also taken its toll on El. She sat next to Reuben on the sofa, and she looked as bad as he did. The good thing was that they had arrived together and appeared to have settled their differences. Newton was still in pain after his encounter with the demons. He held himself stiffly, and Avery could see bandages around his arm and adding bulk under his t-shirt.

They were all weaker than they should be, but they had to act now.

"What have you told her family?" Newton asked.

Avery hesitated, embarrassed. "I told Sam, her husband, that we were doing a late night stock take, and I threw in a little spell to help. It wasn't hard, but it felt horrible."

Avery then told them what she found in her grimoire, and what she and Alex had discovered about the pentagram over White Haven and the centre where the spell had been performed.

"That's where you're confusing me," El cut in. "How can we break the binding spell when we don't have part of the spell—the portion for water?"

"Because we have Helena."

A chorus of "*What?*" echoed around the room.

"She's here with me now. I can feel her. She smells of violets, and she wants us to do this. She made the spell. She *knows* the spell. She doesn't need a grimoire to recite it."

"So that's what I can sense," Alex said thoughtfully. "I thought I was imagining it."

Newton looked spooked. "She's here? *Now?*" He looked around, as if she would materialise next to him.

"I can't see her, Newton," Avery said, trying to reassure him. "It's her presence, her spirit. I *feel* her."

Alex interrupted, "Avery, you know I trust you, I do, and I believe you. But she's a spirit. She has no corporeal body. How can she take part in a spell?"

"Because, Alex, you control the essence of spirit. You have the grimoire. You said yourself it has spells to summon spirits. But she's *already* here. You must know a spell to allow her to enter my body, and then I'll have her knowledge to perform the spell. Reuben can perform the air part of the spell, my part, and I'll do his."

Briar answered first. "That sounds incredibly dangerous, Avery."

"It's Helena, she won't hurt me. Alex?"

For a second he didn't speak, and just stared at her. "Briar's right. It *is* dangerous. And it won't work like that. If she enters your body, your mind will be pushed out of the way—*she'll* control *you*!"

Avery faltered for a second. *That sounded unpleasant, but …* "It will be fine. I trust her."

Alex persisted. "What if you can't get rid of her, what if she sends you mad?"

"It won't. She won't. I feel her. She's gentle and fair—she won't hurt me."

"You don't *know* her, Avery, so you don't know that. And what if the spell goes wrong?"

"So there is one?"

He sighed. "Yes, there is. You would need to surrender your spirit to hers, to allow her in. But I'm scared she would take over, smother you. Then you'd be lost. *Forever.* I don't want that to happen."

It felt as if they were the only two in the room. She felt the others watching them, but she didn't care. "I promise I'll come back."

"You better." He finally broke his gaze and turned to his grimoire on the floor in front of him.

"So it's decided, then." Briar said, her tone even, but her face tense. "I need to prepare my ingredients. My part requires a lot of herbs. What about everyone else's?"

"Mine requires half a dozen," Avery said. "I've already brought them with me. Reuben's, El's and Alex's are incantations only. As my grimoire is the key to the spell, it describes the preparation of the space, too. It seems to be the usual circle of protection. It also describes the order of the incantations to break the spell. It's precise. You need to be familiar with it."

"I presume we're doing this *now*?" El asked.

"We have to," Avery said. She checked her watch. "It's already past six—that only gives us six hours in which to break the spell and get to Faversham's place."

"How?" Reuben asked, looking around at them all. Dark circles were under his eyes, and it looked as if he hadn't slept in days. "You say the centre of the pentagram is where the Church of All Souls is. But *where* in the Church? How do we find it?"

"You're happy to help, then?" El asked him curiously.

"Of course I am. I'm grieving, not useless," he said brusquely.

El flinched, but then he reached out his hand and placed it on hers in apology.

"Right," Avery said, feeling like she needed to get things moving. "Let's check the spells and all the ingredients, and start preparing them here. We'll have to cast the spell that allows Helena in later, at the place where we break the binding. I better go and find it."

"So," Newton said, "what can I do?"

"You can help me find the place."

"Yes, good, I can do that," he agreed, eager to be doing something practical.

"But then what?" Reuben persisted. "Say we're successful, and we break the spell. A demon and a vengeful sprit will then be released. Have we a plan for that?"

"I can handle those, with help," Alex said. "I've been studying the spells in my grimoire like a mad man. And hopefully, if Helena is right, our powers will be released and that will give us some juice."

"She said *unleashed*. That sounds pretty big," Briar said.

"Well, it will be interesting," Alex allowed with a sigh.

"And then we head to Faversham Central and rescue Sally. And your grimoire, Reuben." Avery felt adrenalin rush through her. "And it will give me great pleasure to show daddy Faversham where he can stick his threats."

19

Avery stood next to Newton in front of the Church of All Souls. Its medieval architecture squatted above them, and despite the warmth of the evening, Avery felt a shiver run through her.

The church was typical of its type, with gothic arched windows, a spire, gargoyles and strange, mythical images of the green man on the stonework, and a deep porch with heavy oak doors. It sat just up from an intersection, and it had a small slabbed square in front of it, handy for those attending weddings and funerals to loiter in.

It was still light, and tourists and locals alike were strolling through the town on their way to restaurants and bars. This time last night Avery was one of them, and now she wondered if she ever would be again.

The church doors were still open, allowing late-night worshippers to enter, and Avery and Newton slipped through into the gloom beyond.

All Souls was shadowy and silent, and the temperature plummeted several degrees as they stepped inside the cool confines of the thick walls. Apart from a couple of people who sat near the front in silent contemplation, the church was empty.

Newton looked as serious as she'd ever seen him, and seeing his worried profile, she wondered how he would manage tonight.

"How are you feeling, Newton?"

"Like I'm about to embark on one of the stupidest things I've ever done," he said quietly.

"You don't have to be here. We can manage without you. In fact, you are violating your true role. You're supposed to be stopping us."

He turned and looked at her, his eyes dark and troubled. "That was before I knew the truth of what your families had done and why. I'm also supposed to be protecting you—that's what Peter wanted, too. And besides, the more power you have, the less we have to fear from the Favershams."

"Thank you. We appreciate your support."

"Just promise me you know what you're doing."

She felt doubt surge through her again. "I think we do. But you know we've never done anything like this before."

"You're putting yourself at great risk, Avery."

"My friend Sally's in greater risk than me," she said, hoping that Faversham was true to his word and keeping her safe for now.

He looked around the dark interior of the church. "Well, we'd better find the place, hadn't we? Any thoughts?"

"The crypt," she suggested, thinking about her conversation with Alex. "It's the only place it can be—or at least a place accessed from there."

It was a large church, and they walked down the nave towards the altar, keeping to the aisle on the left, their footsteps echoing around them. They passed the transepts and headed into a small chapel also on the left, out of sight from the visitors.

"Where now?"

Avery pointed to where a narrow, rectangular hole was cut into the floor behind the choir. It was edged with an ornate iron railing to stop people from falling in, and a set of steps led down into darkness.

Looking around cautiously, they made sure no one could see them, and made their way to the entrance.

"Where's the vicar?" Newton whispered.

Avery shrugged. "In his private rooms?"

Avery went to lead the way down, but Newton stopped her. "Let me."

With every step down, the temperature plunged lower and lower until Avery was shivering. At the bottom was a solid oak door, black with age, the arcane face of a gargoyle carved on it. It was locked.

Avery stepped past Newton and laid her hand on the lock, whispering a short spell. The lock released, and she pressed down on the iron handle, swinging the door open.Beyond was only darkness. Avery sent a witch light into the room and then they stepped inside, shutting the door behind them.

They stood on the edge of the long, low roofed room, the walls, floor, and ceiling made of heavy stone blocks. Vaulted archways ran the length of the room, and stone sarcophagi were placed along either side the central aisle. Halfway across the room was another iron railing with a locked gate. Beyond were objects of value—silver chalices and candlesticks.

The crypt was damp and musty, as well as bitingly cold.

At the far end of the room, on the rear wall beyond the railings, was a sign illuminated only by the witch light. It was a large sigil with several lines of runes beneath it.

"Well, at least we know where to look," Newton said. "Isn't it a bit obvious to mark the place?"

Avery shook her head. "The sigil both warns and offers entry, but only to those who are worthy."

"What do you mean?"

"It requires one of us, from the old families, to open it."

Avery walked forward, as if in a trance. With another whispered spell, she opened the locked gate in the middle of the railing and headed to the sigil.

Close up, it exuded power and fear. The mark was complex, but around it, the witch light showed the edges of a door, shimmering with a pale, unearthly light.

"Can you see that?" Avery asked.

Newton nodded. "I can feel it, too. What do the runes say?"

Avery hesitated for a minute as she translated them, glad she'd been researching them recently.

By Air and Fire, Water and Earth, declare your spirit to me.
If I find you worthy, I give entrance to thee.
But if you fail, forever will your soul condemned to misery be.
Are you ready? Declare yourself, and set your powers free.

Avery swallowed. "Well, I think that's pretty clear, don't you?" She turned to Newton. "Stand back. I have no idea quite what will happen."

Newton gave her a long, worried look and then stepped back several paces until he was beyond the railings.

Avery pressed her hands against the sigil.

For a few seconds, nothing happened, but then faint lines like fire began to radiate out from her hands, lighting up every swirling line and mark of the sigil. A tingle spread up Avery's arms and across her chest, radiating down her whole body, just as it was across the sign.

And then it started to burn.

She cried out, and Newton shouted, "What's happening?"

But Avery could barely speak she was so wracked with pain. She was aware of Newton starting to move towards her and she summoned her reserves of strength, shouting, "Stay back!"

The burning intensified until it felt as if her veins and her brain were on fire. Her vision started to dim, and blackness encroached on all sides, until only the sigil remained in front of her, filling her vision.

Her hands were now welded to it, and it seemed to be accessing her mind, pulling out all her secrets. Images flashed across her vision—Alex, her mother, her grandmother, the grimoires, and lastly, Caspian Faversham.

She tried to calm her breathing. This was a test, like it had been for Alex and El. She was pure; she was a descendant of Helena. She deserved to be here. It was her destiny.

And as she thought of Helena, Avery felt her burning-hot flesh flash icy cold for a second, and she became aware of a figure next to her. Avery tore her gaze from the sigil and saw Helena standing next to her.

For a few seconds, Helena's image was translucent, and then it solidified.

Helena was beautiful. Her hair was long and dark, cascading down her back in a thick wave. She was wrapped in a dark cloak, and her face above it was pale. But her eyes shone with fierce desire as she studied Avery.

The smell of violets was strong now, as was the sickening smell of ashes and smoke, and Avery felt herself wretch. She could smell burning flesh, and it was growing stronger by the second, but she held on, willing herself to stay standing and not pass out.

The sigil was now blazing with a fiery light. Avery felt as if her soul was being sucked out of her body. She hung on with every fibre of her being, refusing to give in.

And then it was over. The sigil released her, and she fell to the floor.

With a whisper, the doorway cracked open around the edges and then swung open, and Helena stepped past her into the room without a backward glance.

Within seconds, Newton was at Avery's side.

"Are you okay?"

For a few seconds she couldn't speak, but slowly, the burning subsided and her brain started to function again as her vision cleared. She nodded, taking deep, calming breaths. "Yes, I think so."

Newton's reassuring hands were on her arms, and he helped pull her to her feet.

"Can you see Helena?" Avery asked.

Newton glanced into the room that had been revealed beyond the sigil. "Yes, but barely. She's a ghostly apparition."

Following his gaze, Avery murmured. "Not to me. It's like she's truly flesh and blood."

As if Helena could hear them, she turned and looked at Avery, her eyes burning in her pale face. Her cloak had fallen open, and Avery saw that she wore a long, dark dress with a tight bodice, but then she turned away, dismissing her, and surveyed the room. The feeling of comfort she had given Avery earlier had gone.

Avery felt fear spreading through her. She was about to let this woman into her body.

"I have a very bad feeling about this," Newton hissed.

"Come on. This is no time for doubts," Avery said, trying to subdue her own as she led the way into the room.

Immediately beyond the hidden doorway, a series of shallow steps dropped down to a lower level. As Avery crossed the threshold, light sprang up everywhere, illuminating the magnificent chamber.

Dozens of large-columned candles filled the corners, ran along the walls, lined the aisles, and decorated the altar, revealing the ceiling of vaulted stone, supported by ornate stone columns that formed two rows on either side of the central space.

In the centre of the floor was a giant pentacle—a pentagram, surrounded by a double circle. It was made from different coloured stones—granite, and a red stone that Avery couldn't identify. The signs for the five elements were also marked onto the floor, and in the centre of the pentagram was a devil's trap.

Two large braziers were placed on either side of the altar against the far wall, and they blazed with fire.

Avery could feel the potent magic and power in the room. It resonated with it, caressing her body. It seemed to whisper in her ear like a lover, and she could swear she felt lips on her skin.

She shivered, and it wasn't just from the bone-chilling cold in the room that caused her breath to puff out in white clouds.

Keeping her distance from Helena, who walked with an unearthly grace across the far side of the room, Avery walked around the pentagram to the altar, closely followed by Newton.

"This place is terrifying." Newton said, his face bleak. "It makes my flesh crawl."

"Mine, too," Avery agreed softly, wondering if Helena could hear and understand them.

She turned her attention to the altar, her breath catching as she saw a large jar filled with a swirling black liquid that moved all on its own.

"What's that?" Newton said, eyeing it suspiciously.

"I have a horrible feeling that's Octavia."

"And her demon?"

"Trapped within that, I suspect," she said, pointing to the huge devil's trap in the centre of the pentagram.

Hesitantly, Avery touched the other objects on the altar. They were the usual array of a goblet, bowl, ritual knife, and the powdered remains of what Avery presumed were herbs.

She felt the icy prickle return to her skin, and realised Helena was just to her right, a triumphant smile on her face as she stroked the glass jar. She lifted her head and looked at Avery, sending a shiver to the depths of her soul. And then she turned to Newton, narrowed her eyes, and rushed towards him, causing Newton to stagger back in fear.

But Helena was powerless, and she passed through him, causing Newton to clutch at his chest in shock.

Helena turned back to them, her eyes smouldering with resentment. She was trying to speak, but couldn't, and Avery saw more fury cross her features, transforming her into a witch from the storybooks. And then her anger evaporated, and it was just Helena again.

Avery realised she was holding her breath and she slowly released it, grabbing Newton's arm for comfort.

Newton straightened and breathed easier again, but his face was white.

Avery placed herself in front of him and squared up to Helena. "Things have changed, Helena. Peter Newton never forgave himself for what happened to you. His descendants have helped us through the years!"

Helena cast a resentful glance at Newton, but nodded.

"Will you help us today? Help us break the spell and return our power to us? All five families will be here, but we need your help. The Favershams remain strong, and we cannot fight them without more magic. They already have the Jackson's grimoire. Can you remember the spell for water? Reuben Jackson will swap places, and say the spell for air."

Helena nodded, a malevolent gleam once more springing onto her face. She may not be able to speak, but she understood. She reached out and placed her hand on Avery's arm, and a charge like an electric shock rocketed through Avery. With searing clarity she knew Helena agreed, and she had transmitted one final instruction, as if it was burnt on her brain.

I will lead.

Avery breathed a sigh of relief. She had felt Helena's agreement before, but it was good to have it confirmed. She turned to Newton, a stone in the pit of her stomach. "Go and phone the others. Tell them we're ready."

20

The rest of the group arrived within half an hour, having slipped into the now closed church and down into the crypt.

They were laden with their grimoires and the herbs required to break the binding.

As they stepped into the chamber, their eyes widened, and Alex whistled. "Wow. This is pretty impressive!" He saw Helena standing by the altar and gasped. "I can see Helena."

Helena turned and appraised him, a slow smile spreading across her face, and then she looked at Reuben, El, and Briar standing next to him. Her gaze returned to Reuben, her eyes narrowing speculatively, and then they settled on Alex.

Helena desired Alex, Avery could tell; she looked again at Avery, and a knowing smile crossed her face.

Another chill ran through Avery. She had the feeling that once Helena was in her body, she wasn't going to want to leave it. She subdued the thought. She needed to trust Helena. She was going to save them all.

"Can anyone else see her?" Alex asked.

"A ghost, only barely visible," El said, echoing Newton earlier.

"Same for me," Reuben and Briar agreed.

"I can see her far more clearly," Alex said, looking at Helena warily. "It's not the first time I've seen spirits, but she is far more…" he struggled for words.

"Solid?" Avery suggested.

He nodded, and they both watched Helena pacing up and down, impatient to begin.

"I don't like this *at all*," Briar said, pulling her herbs from her bag. "I don't trust her."

"We haven't got much choice," Avery said. She turned to Alex. "Any tips for expelling a spirit from my body?"

Alex grabbed her hands. "Stay strong. Remember who you are. Hold tight to cherished memories." He pulled her close and kissed her, taking her breath away.

"Guys, get a room!" Reuben said, smirking.

"Sod off, Reuben," Alex said, breaking away and pulling his own grimoire from his pack.

Avery tried to ignore the tingle on her lips. "According to this," she said, reading the instructions in her own grimoire, "we all stand on our respective points of the pentagram. I need to place the glass jar next to the devil's trap. Helena has already indicated to me that she'll lead, so just do what she says. Have you all had a chance to study the spell?"

They nodded, and El clutched the red gemstone necklace that she had been gifted in her wooden box. "I'm as ready as I'll ever be."

"Where should I stand?" Newton asked.

"Just out of this room," Alex suggested. "In the doorway. I suspect that when we start the spell, the demon in that devil's trap will manifest, and it might even get out. Keep well out of the way."

"In fact," Briar said, "maybe you should wait in the church, just in case the vicar comes to call?"

Newton nodded in agreement. "I'll wait in the small side chapel."

"I've brought something for you, just in case," Reuben said, reaching into his sports bag for a large object wrapped in a blanket. He unrolled it to reveal a shotgun and a box of shells.

"Where the hell did you get that?" Newton asked, alarmed.

"Don't worry, we're licensed. We keep it on the estate. The shells are filled with salt."

Alex nodded and laughed. "So that's what you went back for. Good idea."

"Is it?" Newton asked, taking the gun from him and inspecting it.

"Yes. Salt repels spirits, just in case a certain someone needs a reminder of who's in charge." Reuben nodded towards Helena. "Can you use it?"

"I've had firearms training," Newton nodded. "Right then. If you need me, shout."

While they had been preparing, the power in the room seemed to shift and change, as if the energy was rising.

"I can feel the anticipation, can you?" El asked as she took her place on the pentagram.

"Like a charging battery," Reuben agreed, squaring his shoulders. He looked more animated than he had in days.

Apart from Briar, they had all dressed in jeans and boots and jackets, ready for combat. El was wearing her black leather trousers and looked like the angel of death with bright white hair flowing down her back.

Briar, however, still wore her long, flowing clothes, and now she slipped her shoes off, standing barefoot on the cold stones. She saw them watching her. "It grounds me," she explained.

"What do I do about Helena?" Avery asked Alex, once she had moved the glass jar to the right place.

"Stand ready on the Water element sign," he said, bringing a small potion bottle out of his bag and then walking over to join her. "This potion will drug your senses, but only slightly," he added, seeing Avery's alarmed expression. "It will be like when we spirit-walked. There are a few words you need to say, an invocation, to invite her in. Are you sure you want to do this?" Helena was now standing next to Avery, an eager, hungry expression on her face.

Avery summoned her courage. "Yes. We have no choice."

"We do have a choice. We could tackle the Favershams without extra power."

"We'd fail and you know it," she said, casting a wary glance at Helena.

Helena hadn't tried to communicate since they had first arrived, and the sense of calm that she'd first given Avery had now completely gone. Instead, Avery felt Helena resented her, rather than supported her.

Alex took one final worried look at Helena, and then gave Avery a slip of paper he'd written the spell on. It was only a few lines, and she read through them quickly.

"All good," she nodded encouragingly, and Alex returned to his place on Spirit, the point of the pentacle closest to the altar and directly to her left.

She took a long look around the room, taking in the hundreds of candles, the bright braziers, now giving off a smoky heat, and the long shadows from the stone pillars supporting the ceiling, and hoped this would not be the last room she ever knew. Finally, she looked at Helena.

They were strikingly similar, other than the colour of their hair and eyes. They were the same height with small, slim builds, and both had pale skin, but Helena's eyes burned with a fierce desire that Avery wasn't sure she was equal to. Nevertheless, she drank the potion Alex had prepared.

It scorched her throat, and she coughed as the liquid burnt its way down into her stomach. She tasted cinnamon and blackberries, then something peppery and sharp, and then something acrid.

No. That was Helena she could smell.

The scent of burning flesh was back, and smoke now seemed to swirl around Helena as she stood barely an arm's length from Avery, fixing her with a piercing stare. Avery's vision started to swim, and she looked down at the note, quickly saying the words of the spell while she still could.

As soon as they were uttered, she felt her consciousness recede, slipping back into some distant part of her being.

Avery felt Helena ease into her, turning and twisting her way into her body. It was like a cool breeze was running through her veins and tickling her skin. For a few seconds it was pleasant, and then her mind was filled with hundreds of images, some too swift to focus on, others searing in their intensity—particularly one.

The sharp, bitter fear of being dragged to the stake, stumbling on unwilling legs. Anger and the desire for vengeance was so strong that she felt she could almost break free. But the men holding her were too big, their grip like iron around her arms. In a second she was tied to the stake, a huge pyre prepared below her. The firebrands touched the wood and flared beneath her.

Avery tried to scream, but couldn't, her mouth clamped shut by Helena. And then the image was gone, replaced by the memories of her nights with Alex. She could feel Helena examining them minutely, and if Avery could have blushed, she would, but then that disappeared, too.

Avery now started to panic. She felt suffocated; crushed beneath Helena's mind and her considerable will.

If Helena was aware of Avery's panic, she didn't show it, instead focussing on the room and the need to perform the spell.

Avery saw the room through her eyes, the other witches standing ready, looking nervous but determined. She felt Helena's excitement, but also her annoyance and disappointment. She looked down on them and their lack of knowledge, she could feel it simmering in her. Except for Alex. She *wanted* him.

As if Helena suddenly became aware of Avery's presence, she mentally shoved her, and it took all of Avery's concentration to hold on. It was as if she was trying to displace her from her own body.

Alex spoke. Avery could see his lips move, but she couldn't hear him. It seemed as if she was under water.

"I am ready. Are you?" Helena asked. Her words came out of Avery's mouth, making Avery's skin crawl. And it seemed to repel the others, too. They all took one long look at her, glanced at each other, and then nodded.

Helena began.

She spoke the words of the spell cleanly and with authority, her voice growing stronger as she progressed. She never faltered once, and she nodded at each of the others in turn when it was their time to join in.

Power was building in the room, and as the spell was uttered and repeated, each part layered on top of each other, line by line, full of intention and conviction, the devil's trap began to glow with a strange, blue light.

The shape of a demon rose up from the floor, streaming like smoke through a vent, and at the same time, an awful, gut-wrenching growl rumbled around the room.

Helena's excitement began to rise and she pointed her finger—Avery's finger—at the glass jar, which sat a short distance from the devil's trap, and uttered a final command.

The swirling liquid became agitated, speeding up like a whirlpool, until the jar rocked violently and fell over, smashing instantly, the liquid spreading over the stone. A shriek pierced the room, bloodcurdling in its intensity.

And then it seemed as if all hell broke loose.

A wave of sheer power exploded from the centre of the room, throwing all of them off their feet and out of the pentagram.

Avery sailed through the air, and then felt the bone-shaking smack of cold stone at her back, and also Helena's shock. She struggled to breath, wincing at the ache through her entire body, but Helena bounced back to her feet, threw back her head, and called the power to her.

Avery sensed rather than saw it, feeling a rush of power flood through her with such force that her spirit left her body with a jolt, thrown up to the roof above them.

She had a moment of shock as she saw her body below her, now possessed by Helena. The silver cord attaching her to her body curled below her, swaying in the power that had rocketed around the room.

Avery realised she had a birds-eye view of the action below. She could see the aura of magical energy spiralling around the room like a tornado, all different shades of reds, blues, purples, oranges and greens. The different colours were honing in on the different witches, flowing into them. All five witches now stood tall, with their heads thrown back and mouths wide open as the magic poured into them.

In the centre of the pentagram, the demon and Octavia continued to form into their full shapes, as the powerful bonds that had contained them disappeared.

But there was too much energy to be contained in the small room. Avery saw it flood out the door and up through the ceiling, and she followed it, passing through the church and out into the night air.

In the skies above White Haven, a dark purple mass rippled out across the town like a tidal wave, and the giant pentagram that connected the town to this point sparked like fuse wire.

For a few moments, Avery watched, mesmerised, as the magical energy poured into the night, hanging on the air and casting a veil over the town.

Below, people on the street looked around in shock, as if they had heard or seen something, but then with a shrug, they carried on, and Avery realised they subconsciously may have registered something happening, but they had no idea what.

Avery hovered above the church, her cord streaming below her. They had released something fundamental tonight, she could feel it in her spirit body, and with a sense of excitement, but no little worry, she wondered what the consequences would be.

And then Avery experienced a short, sharp tug on her cord and with a feeling of dislocation, she instantly knew Helena was trying to sever her cord.

21

Avery focussed on her physical body and rushed back to the crypt below.

She found a scene of chaos.

The demon had now broken free of the devil's trap and was lashing the room with whips of flame. It was huge, bigger than any they had seen before. Its form was rippling and changing, and it was impossible to predict what it would do next. Alex was desperately trying to subdue it, his lips moving furiously in a chant, his arms outstretched, the other three witches supporting him.

Helena was fully occupied with fighting Octavia, who now appeared unnervingly fully formed. Avery presumed that like Helena, her spirit form had manifested very strongly. Octavia was an imposing woman, with long, white hair streaming over her shoulders and a face full of fury. They were attacking each other with every elemental force they could summon, which was fortunate for Avery because while Helena was engaged with Octavia, she couldn't try to kill her. Because as much as she hated to admit it, that was exactly what Helena was trying to do.

Avery tried not to panic. She focused on being back in her body, but Helena had blocked her in some way; she could see a shield all around her body. How had she done that? Avery could also see a black mark on her life cord. If that severed, she was dead. As the two ancient witches fought,

Avery noticed that with every hit Helena took, the shield wavered. That was her chance.

She watched her friends, who were finally getting the demon under control. While Briar and Reuben contained the demon within a magical force field, a doorway started to whirl open in the air behind it, and through it Avery could see the world beyond. Her spirit body could see more than her physical one, and she reeled back in shock. Thousands of tormented and vengeful spirits were pushing at the doorway and some even sneaked out, fleeing the room. They had to close the doorway before more escaped. But before she could think of how to warn them, Octavia blasted Helena with a tornado of air and she flew across the room, collapsing against the wall. The shield wavered and vanished, and Avery streamed back into her body.

Avery could feel Helena's shock and rage—now directed at her *and* Octavia, but as Octavia was still attacking her, Helena could not attack Avery. Avery could also feel the potency of her newfound magic. For a second she found it overwhelming, and then she took advantage and attacked Helena, too, trying to force her out of her body.

For what seemed like minutes, but was probably only seconds, their spirits wrestled as Octavia advanced on them.

Avery was vaguely aware of movement in her peripheral vision, and then Newton appeared, his shotgun raised. He aimed at Octavia and blasted her, sending her flying backwards. He fired again, and then reloaded.

Avery now felt Helena's panic and she yelled, "*Get out of my body!*" She had no idea if she really was shouting, or it was all in her head.

Helena seethed and shouted back, "*No! I died before my time. I will have vengeance!*"

"You have had your time, Helena. You made your sacrifice." Avery was so incensed that Helena was trying to kill her that her anger made her stronger, and with one final, furious push, she ejected Helena.

Relief flooded though her. But Helena stood before her, her face twisted with anger, and she again tried to force her way in. And then a blast sounded to her left, and Helena's spirit wavered and flickered. She turned to see Newton striding towards her, and once again he blasted Helena, shattering her this time into thousands of pieces.

"Get rid of Octavia!" he shouted. "I'll keep Helena under control."

Avery ran on shaky legs over to Octavia, who was now struggling to stand. With a well-timed blast of air, she sent her backwards again. But Octavia regained control quickly and flew at her, hundreds of years of anger fuelling her magic.

In a surprising show of physical force, Octavia dragged Avery to the floor and placed a hand on her chest. Avery felt an icy cold spread through her body. She couldn't breathe, and the more she tried to inhale, the worse the pain got.

Then Avery caught a glimpse of the demon over Octavia's shoulder.

It was being sucked back into the spirit world, the doorway swirling behind it. But it wasn't going alone. With one final lash of his fiery whips, he caught Octavia and dragged her with him. Avery could breathe again.

With a word of command from Alex, the doorway collapsed and disappeared, and the demon and Octavia vanished, with only her echoing scream to remind them she had ever been there.

Newton shouted. "What do you want to do with this one?"

Still gasping for air, Avery rolled over and saw Newton standing over Helena's writhing spirit form, gun pointing down at her.

Alex ran over. "Let me." But before he could act, Helena vanished from sight.

"Where the hell has she gone?" Newton shouted, spinning around.

"No idea," Alex said, "but she won't come back for a while."

"You might have to keep a loaded shotgun in your flat," Newton said to Avery.

"We'll find another way to deal with her," Alex decided. He turned to Avery, his eyes narrowed. "Are you okay?"

"I'm fine, now," she said, sitting up. "Things were a bit scary for awhile there. What about you?"

"Feeling like I could do this all night," Alex said. "That hit of magic was intense!"

Reuben, El, and Briar joined them. All of them looked slightly battered. Their hair was ruffled, dirt was streaked over Reuben where he'd fallen to the floor, and El was cradling her arm where Avery could see a burn.

El grinned, "Alex is right. The power that flooded into us was insane. It feels like it's ebbing slightly, but wow, it was amazing."

Briar agreed, "It's like it's woken up some magical knowledge. Some of the spells from the original grimoire actually make sense to me now."

"It's definitely woken up my magic," Reuben said, rubbing his head. "And yours, Alex. Where the hell did you get the spell from?"

"The doorway spell?" Alex grinned. "Like you say, I was juiced up on magic, and the knowledge just flooded into me."

Newton shook his head. "Well, I couldn't see anything, but I sure could feel something. It was like a wave rippled through the town. If I hadn't known what was going on here, I probably would have dismissed it—like I was imagining something. But clearly, I wasn't."

"Well, there's plenty I can tell you about that," Avery said, "but we have somewhere to be. Are you ready for round two?"

"There's no way that going to Faversham Central can be as bad as this," Reuben said, looking around the crypt.

"I wouldn't bet on it." Avery hedged. "Newton, you'd better come, too. You're pretty handy with that shotgun."

"It's got salt in it, not real shotgun pellets."

Reuben reached into his pocket and pulled out another box. "Proper ones. Just in case."

Newton glared. "I'm a police officer—I'm not going to kill anyone. And neither are you."

"We don't know what we're going to face. Take them."

Newton reluctantly accepted the shells.

"And why are you shooting Helena?" El asked. "I thought she was your friend?"

"That was before she tried to steal my body, but I'll catch you up later. Are we all ready?"

"Yep, let's go." Alex led the way out of the hidden crypt, and as Avery crossed the threshold, the chamber plunged into darkness and sealed itself shut.

22

The group arrived at Sebastian Faversham's mansion, and parked up the lane, well out of view.

He lived in a large Tudor dwelling on the edge of Harecombe, very similar in style to Greenlane Manor, edged with a high brick wall.

They clambered over the wall and landed under the trees on the far side of the garden. The house was visible a short distance away, the windows mainly dark, other than a few on the ground and first floor, and a variety of cars were assembled on the drive in front of the house.

"So, what's the plan?" Reuben asked, checking out the grounds nervously.

"Find Sally first and get her out of here, and then we get the grimoire," Avery said.

"How do we find her?" Reuben asked. "That's a big house."

"I've come prepared. She has a hairbrush at work. I've taken her hair and made a locator spell. I'll release it as soon as we're in the house—we'll just have to follow the light. And then one of us needs to whisk her to safety."

"I can do that," Newton volunteered. "I'll bring her back to the van."

"But how the hell do we find the grimoire?" Alex asked. "There's no locator spell for *that*."

"I'm sure we'll think of something. The important thing is to get Sally out safely."

As Briar finished speaking, a howl set up across the grounds.

"What's that?" Newton said, raising his gun.

"Crap! Dogs," Alex said, pointing to half a dozen animals racing across the grounds towards them.

The dogs spread out in a line, snarling and snapping. They had a feral green glow to them, were twice the size of normal dogs, and as they drew closer, their large canines glinted in the garden lights.

"Oh great, not just any dogs," Avery said, getting ready to defend herself. "I think we've set off a magical alarm system."

"So much for a stealthy approach," Briar said. "Leave the dogs to me. You all head to the house, and I'll catch you later."

Briar was still barefoot, and she planted herself firmly, squaring her shoulders as she uttered a spell. With a juddering shake, the ground cracked open in front of the dogs, and they started to fall in, howling and yelping, but the others didn't stop to watch.

They ran to a ground floor window at the back of the house, well away from the brightly-lit ones.

"There's a spell on the entrances," El said, touching the wood tentatively. "It looks complex."

"Well, we'd better break it soon, because some of those dogs are still loose and they're heading this way," Reuben warned, turning to face them. He directed a blast of energy at the closest dog, and it collapsed on the ground.

"I'll just *fry* the spell," El said, now confident. She placed her hand on the necklace she had inherited with her grimoire.

"This seems to store elemental fire, and it's super juiced up at the moment."

She slipped her necklace off and held the stone on the glass. For a brief second it illuminated the web of spells protecting the house, and then flames raced across the window, breaking the spell and shattering the glass all at once.

They knocked the rest of the glass out, piled into the room, and then raced to the door.

Before they opened it, Avery brought Sally's hair out of her pocket. It was stored in a small cotton bag and wrapped with twine. She whispered a spell over it, and it blossomed into a tiny blue light.

For a second the light just bobbed in the air, and then it passed through the door and they hurried to follow it.

Beyond was a passageway, and the light led them down to the main part of the house. They had only gone a few paces when a familiar, dark-haired woman appeared in a whirl of air and magic. It was Estelle, Caspian's sister.

Estelle was statuesque, with long, dark hair and compelling eyes. She was dressed head to foot in black and her arms were outstretched, blocking the passage and ready to attack. Her face was triumphant. "So, you dared to come here with your pathetic powers? You're more foolish than we thought. Did you think you could enter our house and we wouldn't know?"

Avery stepped forward, eager to wipe the smile off her face. "Of course you would know, but we don't scare that easily."

Estelle narrowed her eyes. "Well, you're even more stupid than I thought." And without warning she sent a cloud of black smoke at them. It quickly billowed around them, blinding them all as it grew thicker and more impenetrable.

Avery's eyes burned, and for the second time that evening, she struggled to breathe.

But someone reacted equally quickly, and she heard Estelle shout out in pain. In seconds, the black smoke disappeared, and Avery saw El's flaming sword skewered through Estelle's side. Reuben didn't hesitate; he sent a bolt of energy at the ceiling above Estelle, bringing plaster and a large beam of wood down on her head. She fell unconscious on the floor below.

"That was easier than I thought," Reuben said, pulling El's sword free and passing it back to her. "Good aim, El."

"Lucky shot, really," she grimaced.

They stepped over to Estelle's body, and El conjured a fiery rope to wrap around Estelle's prone form. They dragged her into a side room and sealed the door.

The blue light bobbed ahead of them, and they quickly followed it along another side corridor, into the depths of the house. The house was furnished with impeccable taste, and they progressed quietly down the carpeted corridors lined with priceless works of art.

A shout disturbed them, and they turned to find two men they hadn't met before, but had only seen on photos; Caspian's cousins, Hamish and Rory, one blond and the other dark-haired.

As Avery quickly assessed their opposition, she was aware of movement behind her. She turned to find Caspian grinning malevolently. They were trapped.

The next few minutes were a jumble of shouts, wind, fire, and water, and they summoned every bit of power they had. El's sword flashed with fire, balls of energy bounced off the walls, and then the lights went out.

Avery wasn't sure if they were winning or not. The energy balls pummelled her, and several times she fell before getting up again. She realised she had been separated from the others, and suddenly Caspian loomed above her.

Just as Avery was about to throw up a protective shield, the floor cracked and rumbled, and Caspian also lost his balance, falling on top of Avery. She could feel his hot breath on her face, and his weight crushed her.

Briar was here, somewhere.

Massive roots shot up through the floor of the mansion, wrapping around Caspian's ankles and pulling him through the splintered floor and down into the ground.

His face was masked in fury, and he turned and tried to blast the roots free. Some he did manage to break, but the rest were too strong.

Avery was caught up with him, unable to break free, and once Caspian realised it he sneered, grabbed her tight, and pulled her with him.

Avery waited for the horrible, suffocating feeling of earth to cover her, but instead, they fell through space, crashing onto a stone floor below.

The smells of damp and mould were overwhelming. They were in the cellars.

She had fallen on Caspian, which at least provided her with a soft, if bumpy, landing. She fought free of him and the roots that continued to snake around them. Out of the corner of her eye, she saw the blue light bob away to her right.

Sally.

Newton dropped through the hole in the ceiling next to her, winded, but still holding his shotgun. "Are you okay?"

"Sort of," she said, smashing at another tree root. "Better than him."

Caspian was now wrapped in roots that bound him like iron. Avery could see bright blue flashes that encased his body as he tried to free himself, but so far, he was failing.

"Are they okay up there?" She looked up into the darkness of the corridor above. The sizzle of magic snapped like lightning in the dark, and she caught a flash of El's sword scything through the air.

"As far as I could see. Come on, we have to trust they'll be all right." Newton followed the blue light, leaving Avery with no choice but to follow him.

The guiding light led through several interconnected rooms, all in darkness, until eventually they came to another corridor. The air smelt slightly fresher here, and they saw another light ahead.

A room opened up on their left, with a dim light seeping through a small hatch at eye level in a wooden door. The hatch was lined with iron bars, and they edged to it, ready to fight.

Avery peered through the opening and saw Sally lying on a pallet on the floor. There was no one else in sight. She turned to Newton with relief. "It's Sally, and she's alone."

As she reached for the handle, a snarl came out of the darkness, and a dog launched at both of them, mouth wide and dripping with saliva.

Newton pulled the shotgun up and blasted it, twice. It howled and then fell dead at their feet.

"Quick reflexes, Newton," Avery said admiringly. She called out, "Sally, it's us, we're coming in!"

The door was sealed with a very simple spell, and Avery easily unlocked it as Newton reloaded. Fortunately, the Faversham's arrogance was an asset for them.

Sally sat up, looking confused. Her face was streaked with tears and dirt, her hands were blooded and bruised, and she shivered in the cold. "Avery! Where am I? How long have I been here?"

Avery rushed over and hugged her. "Sally, we'll explain everything later. Are you okay?"

"Yes—no, not really," she said and burst into tears.

"Can you walk?"

"Yes, I'm not hurt." She struggled to her feet.

"What did you do to your hands?' Avery asked, concerned.

"I beat the door and made myself hoarse from shouting, but all I could hear was a bloody great dog."

"Can you remember anything?"

"No! The last thing I remember was being in the shop, and then I woke up here."

"Okay, we need to move. We're getting you out of here. Newton, anything else out there?"

"Not yet!" he called.

"Right, follow me, Sally."

Avery pulled Sally out of the room, and then followed Newton along the corridor until they eventually came to a set of steps leading up. At the top of the stairs, they headed through another door to find that the passage led two ways— one back into the main part of the house, and one to a rear entrance.

"Right, leave Sally with me," Newton said. "Well be waiting in the van."

"Are you sure you can get out of the grounds?"

"I'm pretty sure the family's tied up here. And I can handle dogs." He looked at Sally. "Think you can run?"

Sally's colour had already returned. "Yes, honestly, I'm fine. I'm just glad to be out of that room."

Avery nodded. "All right. I'll see you later. And Newton, if we're not out in an hour, go."

"If you're not out in an hour, I'm coming after you," he said firmly, his eyes glinting fiercely in the dark. And with that he headed out the door with Sally.

Avery turned back toward the interior of the house.

She heard a distant *boom*, and then the house shuddered. Every light went out. *Was that us, or them, doing that?* Avery considered producing a witch light, and then decided against it for now. She edged along the corridor, her eyes slowly adjusting to the darkness. The air changed, and she realised she was entering the large entrance hall, as she saw the broad curve of the stairs next to her. To her right, a long corridor ran away into darkness, and she heard shouts and felt the sizzle of magic. She was about to make her way to it, when a figure ran towards her. She prepared to attack, and then realised it was Alex. He too had his hands raised. He stopped when he saw her and sighed with relief. She ran to the edge of the hall to join him.

"Are you okay?" she whispered.

He nodded. "Rory and Hamish are big thugs and powerful, and then Uncle Rupert waded in. It was touch and go for a while, but we broke free. Briar's coming now, while El and Reuben secure the others."

Over his shoulder she saw Briar's small shape running towards them, grinning as she saw Avery. She was slightly out of breath, but blue flames trickled through her fingers, and she looked raring to go. "Have you found Sally?" she asked, standing next to them.

Avery nodded. "Yeah, and Newton's taken her to the van. Now we just need to find the grimoire."

"Any ideas?"

Avery's shoulders sagged. "Not really."

They fell silent for a few seconds, and then Alex grinned. "What if we used the locator spell with blood? Would it work on Reuben's grimoire?"

"It might do!" Avery said, brightening. "He needed his blood to reveal it; maybe his blood will lead us to it as well."

Alex led them back down the corridor, but they'd only gone a short distance when they met Reuben and El. With their light hair and dark clothes, and El's sword still glowing with fire, they looked like avenging angels. Both of them smelled of singed hair and smoke. Alex pulled them all into an elegant room, lit only by the faint moonlight from outside.

"We need your blood and hair," Alex said to Reuben.

"Now?" Reuben asked, clearly confused. "What for?"

"To find your grimoire." Avery looked sheepish. "I just wish I'd thought of it earlier."

"You know the spell?" Briar asked, from where she stood at the doorway to make sure no one appeared unexpectedly.

"Sure, but it will be basic." Avery turned and grabbed an antique silver bowl from a cabinet. "And this will be perfect."

Reuben pulled a few strands of hair out, and then El gave him her sword. He pulled it across the palm of his hand, and a stream of blood trickled in to the bowl. Avery added the hair and then whispered a spell, holding her hand above it. The blood and hair started to bubble together, and as they mixed, it boiled down to nothing, until only smoke remained in the bowl. The smoke then rose out of the bowl, a deep, blood red glow within it, and drifted in the air for a second. Avery said another spell, "Blood to blood, hair and skin, lead us to the spells of the kin."

The smoke drifted to the door where it hung for a few moments before heading right, back to the main entrance, and then up the grand stairs to the next floor.

"Are you sure the others are tied up?" Avery asked El as they followed the smoke.

"Absolutely. Any sign of Caspian?'

"He's downstairs, Briar looked after him."

"So, just Sebastian, then?" Alex checked, hearing them.

Avery nodded. "I hope so."

At the top of the stairs, the smoke headed down a long corridor, passing several doorways. It moved faster and faster, until it streaked down another corridor, and then through a doorway on their right, where they found themselves in an enormous library.

A glimpse of the moon beyond the window cast the room in a silvery light. As Avery's eyes adjusted, she saw that all four walls were lined with shelves, packed with books. Leather armchairs were placed around the room, and in the centre was a large wooden desk. On it was Reuben's grimoire.

Unfortunately next to it, seated at ease, was Sebastian Faversham. He sat very still, his elbows resting on the arms of the chair, his hands together under his chin as if in prayer.

They pulled up short at the doorway, preparing to defend themselves. But Sebastian just stared at them, his face in shadow.

His voice hissed across the room. "What *have* you done?"

"We have defended ourselves," Avery said, thinking he was referring to their fight.

"I don't mean that!" he said, his voice threatening. "You destroy my house, attack my family, but you have done far worse than that."

Reuben was seething. "You have stolen my book, kidnapped an innocent woman, and *killed* my brother! You dare ask what *we* have done?"

Sebastian slowly rose to his feet, seeming huge in the shadows. "I mean the magic you have released from under All Soul's Church."

"Ah, yes," Avery said, shuffling awkwardly. "You noticed that?"

"Noticed?" His voice rose. "The whole magical community will have noticed! The magic even now pools above White Haven, drawing attention and all manner of creatures."

Avery felt her heart thump loudly. She glanced at the others, but they looked as baffled as she felt. "What do you mean, 'creatures?'"

"Anyone or any *thing* remotely connected to magic will have sensed that today. It rocked this house, and beyond. I hope you're pleased with yourselves."

A thousand possibilities raced through Avery's head, but she subdued them. There was plenty of time to worry about his accusations later. *How dare he presume to be so much better than them!*

"We're pleased we've found our old family magic," Avery said, annoyed and stepping into the room. "If it wasn't for Octavia, it wouldn't have been trapped down there, anyway! Maybe, if there was something to worry about, you should have been more honest."

Alex stood next to her. "No, he's just pissed off because we have just as much power as him."

Sebastian threw back his head and laughed, and the sound sent chills down Avery's spine. "Power! It's not just about power!"

"So, we can have the grimoire then?" Reuben asked.

"You think you're so clever, don't you?" Avery could hear the sneer in Sebastian's voice. He lifted his hands, and flames started to crackle in his palms. "You may have released your magic, but I shall destroy your book, and then you'll see what true power is!"

In a split second, he turned and threw flames at the grimoire, but before any of them could respond, the grimoire flew across the room towards them, smacking Reuben in the stomach and sending him staggering back. His hands wrapped around it, holding it tightly. Briar and El stepped forward on either side of him, preparing to attack.

Avery turned back to Sebastian, wondering what had happened, and then saw the bright, burning image of Helena materialise in front of him. The smell of burning flesh was sharp and nauseating, and smoke poured off Helena's body, filling the room.

If it was an apparition, it was a strong one. Avery covered her nose and mouth and squinted through the smoke. Helena had leapt at Sebastian and wrapped him in her burning body. Whatever magic had been released earlier had strengthened Helena, and she now swelled with power.

Not only did Helena appear to have gained physical form, but Sebastian could clearly feel her, too. As she wrapped herself around him, he screamed with rage and pain.

Avery felt Alex's hand on her arm. "Time to go."

"But..." she looked back to Sebastian, horrified. He was burning alive.

"*Now, Avery*," Alex said, pulling her out the room and down the corridor, running after the others, who raced ahead of them.

The thick, black smoke poured after them, following them like an animal, and they raced down the stairs, out through the front door and across the grass.

Avery risked a look back to the house. She could see the library window from there; it was the only one filled with flames.

23

Newton drove them all back to White Haven as fast as possible without attracting attention. Desperate as they were to get home, he went the long way around, avoiding traffic cameras and anything that might incriminate them in whatever had happened at the manor.

They sat on the floor in the back of the van, propped on old blankets and braced between boxes and the sides, trying not to topple over as Newton steered them to safety.

"Can we please release whatever spells bound the others?" Avery asked, as soon as she could get her breath. "I don't want to think Helena will kill all of them—they don't deserve that."

"I beg to differ," Reuben said, his eyes hard. He still clutched his grimoire.

Briar answered, "Already done. I don't want that either, Avery."

"How the hell did Helena gain physical form?" Reuben asked.

"I'm not sure she really has," Alex explained. "I think it's just a severe and strong manifestation, brought on by the wave of magic we released, and her fury at the Favershams. After all, his ancestor is the reason she was burnt at the stake."

"But the smell," Briar said, covering her face with her hands. "It was awful. I still feel sick."

"Imagine being burnt alive—that would be far worse," El reasoned. "Are you all right, Avery? Things seemed really weird under All Souls when she possessed you."

Avery fell silent for a moment, trying to work through what had happened. "As much as I hate to say it, I don't think she wanted me back in my body. I accidentally spirit walked when the spell broke, so she didn't do that, but she sure didn't want to let me back in, either."

Alex was sitting next to her, and he snaked his arm around her and pulled her close. Avery shivered with pleasure, snuggling into him. He sighed. "I had a horrible feeling that would happen."

"I know you did, but we needed her," Avery said. "And at least we broke the spell, rescued Sally, and got the grimoire."

"But will she come back?" Briar asked. "What if she tries to get back inside you?"

"I let her in last time, remember? I don't think it can happen again."

"I think another tattoo might be in order," Reuben said with a wink.

Avery rolled her eyes. She looked up to the front of the van, where Sally was sitting in the passenger seat next to Newton, silent for now. She called over, "How are you, Sally?"

For a few seconds Sally didn't move, and then she turned around to look at them all, finally resting her gaze on Avery. "I'm not entirely sure, Avery. In fact, I'm not sure of anything at the moment."

Newton called back over his shoulder. "I've been trying to explain a few things to Sally, but—"

She finished the sentence for him. "There's magic, and there's *magic*, and I just need some time for it to soak in. And don't you *dare* think about spelling it out of my head!" She said forcefully.

Avery raised her hands in surrender. "Witches honour—if you'll keep this a secret!"

"Of course I will," Sally snorted as she turned back to look out of the windscreen. "I don't want to be carried off to the local loony bin."

"And how are you, Newton?" Briar asked.

"I'm fine," he said, still concentrating on the road. "Just hoping I can keep us all out of trouble with the police."

"There's no way the Favershams will report it, so I think we'll be fine," El said.

"And what about the magical explosion?" Briar asked. "I think we need to talk about that. We've released something that might have huge consequences."

"Ah, yes," Reuben said. "The *creatures* we will attract to White Haven."

"You know what?" Avery said, "I just want to appreciate having got through tonight. Let's discuss everything else tomorrow night. Meet at mine?"

There were nods of agreement, and then Sally said, "And make me a new hex bag, will you, Avery? Just *way* stronger than the last one."

***

Before Avery went to sleep that night, she sealed her flat tightly with spells of protection—just in case the Favershams decided to retaliate—and then spent some time looking at both of her grimoires.

As she turned the pages, new understanding flooded through her. Spells that she had struggled to really understand and use now made more sense. And with a shock, she found in her new, or rather, *old* grimoire that she would forever call

Helena's, the spell that allowed transformation and flight—the mysterious way that Caspian Faversham could appear out of the air. A shiver of excitement and fear ran through her. She would practice that, and then teach the others. She allowed herself a smile at their victory.

Unable to suppress her increasing yawns, she headed to bed, thinking of Alex. Whatever was now happening between them seemed to be more than just physical. He had looked genuinely worried about her earlier, and sitting in the back of the van with his arm wrapped around her had provoked a feeling of peace and security she hadn't felt in a long time.

But the last thought that flitted through her mind as she drifted to sleep was Sebastian's warning about the *creatures* they might attract, and she wondered if that also included the Council—whoever they were.

***

When Avery woke up the next day, she looked out the window, expecting White Haven to look different. But it didn't. The same people wandered down the winding streets, the sun still rose as normal, and her flat looked the same as it always had.

But, she realised, she felt distinctly different. The power they had released yesterday still coursed through her veins, and she felt a subtle awareness of her surroundings and an awareness of her own abilities more than ever. She thought of the other witches, and wondered if they felt the same.

Despite the late night and her lack of sleep, Avery felt full of energy and she headed down to the shop early, planning to ease her way into the day, but Sally was already there and looking surprisingly well, considering her ordeal. She sat at the small wooden table in the back of the shop

216

with her coffee in front of her, and she looked up as Avery entered.

"Morning, Avery," she smiled. Her blonde hair was in a ponytail, her eyes were bright with curiosity, and Avery realised she was looking at her with new knowledge and awareness that had never existed before.

"Morning, Sally! How are you?" Avery rushed over and pulled her into a hug, making Sally rise awkwardly out of her chair.

"I'm fine." Sally said, a gentle reprimand in her voice. "How are *you*?"

"Good. Very good! But look, I'm so sorry about yesterday, you don't need to be here today. Have the day off—in fact, have the week off," she said in a rush, feeling guilt sweep over her.

"Don't be ridiculous. Sam will wonder what's going on. I don't normally take a week off after a stock take."

Avery grinned sheepishly. "Did he believe it?"

"Completely. I'm not entirely sure I'm comfortable keeping this a secret from him, though."

Avery poured a coffee and sat down opposite Sally. "Do what you need to. I trust your judgement, and I trust Sam."

Sally smiled. "Thanks, Avery. It would make me feel better. Besides, who will I gossip to? *Real* witches in White Haven!"

"But you knew I was a witch!" Avery said, thinking of their conversation the other day.

"Maybe I didn't understand it as well as I do now. And I think it would be a good idea to let Dan in on it, too. Your *magical explosion* last night may be the start of more weird things happening around here."

Avery grinned, pleased to be letting more people into what had been her hidden world. "I agree. Thanks, Sally. I really appreciate that you're not freaking out about this."

"I'm your friend, Avery. And besides, what's life without a little magic?" Sally watched Avery for a second or two, sipping her coffee. "Do you want to tell me what happened last night? All of it?"

"Sure," Avery said with a grin, and she recounted everything in as succinct a way as she could. "Did you feel it? The explosion, I mean?"

Sally shook her head. "I'm afraid not. It must have bypassed us ordinary people. Unless it was because I was locked in a basement."

Avery's shoulders sagged. "Are you sure he didn't hurt you?"

"I am. I was unconscious for most of it."

Avery nodded, and hoped this meant Faversham had some morals. And then she felt a rush of guilt about Sebastian.

"Come on," Sally said, watching her. "Let's open the shop and keep ourselves busy."

The morning passed in the usual way, and as soon as Avery had the chance, she let Dan know what had happened.

They were taking advantage of a quiet moment in the shop, and were both perched behind the counter on stools, nibbling on a pastry. Well, Avery was nibbling on a pastry. Dan had demolished his in two bites.

He looked at her, much as Sally had done, with new knowledge and speculation on his face. "So, does this mean weird old White Haven is going to get weirder?"

"It might," Avery said, shrugging. "Did you feel anything strange last night? It would have been late evening?"

Dan looked thoughtful. "I was in the pub debating life, as normal—"

"You mean football," Avery said, interrupting him.

He adopted a lofty expression and continued, "Debating *life*, sipping on beer, and yes, I might have felt something. Like a ripple of..." He hesitated, puzzled. "I can't quite describe it. It was like a shift of some sort. And then it went."

"A shift?"

He nodded. "Yes, like reality wobbled for a second. But then it went."

Avery looked at him sceptically. "Are you sure you weren't drunk?"

"I may have had a pint or two, but I was not drunk," he said, mock offended.

"Do you think anyone else noticed it?"

"Maybe. For a second some people seemed to look around, and then it just passed."

Avery nodded, thinking about when she had been spirit walking above All Souls and had seen people below on the street. So, some people had felt *something*.

"Thanks, Dan. I hope you still want to work here."

He looked shocked, and then grinned. "Of course I do! This is great!"

24

Reassured after nothing unusual—or more unusual than normal—had happened in the shop or White Haven, Avery locked up at the normal time and went to her flat to prepare for the other witches.

She spent a good hour cleaning and tidying things away, and then organised some food. By the time Alex arrived, the smell of garlic was wafting around her kitchen and living room, and floating out of the open balcony doors, mixing with the smell of incense.

Candles were scattered around the room, and the place looked warm and inviting.

"Hey," Alex said, joining her in the kitchen and plonking a pack of beer down on the counter. His long hair was loose and slightly wild, and his usual day-old stubble was actually looking more like a week's worth.

Avery felt her heart flutter wildly just looking at him. "Hey, you. You're early."

"I know; I wanted to catch you alone before the others arrived."

"Cool," she said smiling. "Any time."

He just watched her for a few seconds, his eyes dark and thoughtful. "You know, you scared the crap out of me last night."

She turned to him, leaning against the counter. "I scared the crap out of myself, too."

"I mean it, Avery. If anything had happened to you, if Helena had killed you or possessed your body, I'm not sure what I'd have done. You mean a lot to me. I just need you to know that." He pulled her towards him, encircling her with his arms, and she looked up at him, willing her heart to behave.

"You mean a lot to me, too."

"The meal the other night, we should do that more."

"I agree. I loved it."

His gaze wandered from her eyes to her lips and back again. "You've always been beautiful. You're one of the reasons I came back to White Haven."

For a second, Avery completely forgot they were standing in her kitchen.

"What? No, I'm not."

"Will you stop telling me what I think? I came back for you. All that time I travelled, something was missing, and then I realised what it was. Look at you. You're unfairly sexy."

She unconsciously patted her head and smoothed her hair. "No, I'm not." She struggled to think of something coherent to say, and failed. "What do you mean, you came back for me?"

He smiled and caught her hand in his. "Stop messing with your hair. I missed you. You *know* me. And these last few weeks have just proven that to me."

"But when we were young, you were so … aloof, half the time."

"So were you. We were teenagers."

Avery had to admit that he was sort of right. "But you've been back for months, and have barely given me a second glance."

"I've given you plenty of second glances, you just didn't see them. Or want to see them. You put up very effective barriers."

She gasped. "Liar!"

"You do. To everyone. You just don't want to admit it." He became suddenly serious. "I mean it. I like this. Us. I want it to work. Do you?"

"Yes, I do," she said, breaking into a broad grin.

"Good," he declared, kissing her and leaving her breathless and with desire stirring deep in her belly. And then the bang of the outside door broke them apart, and the others arrived with a clatter of chatter, wine, and beer.

They sat around the table, talking for hours about the events of the previous night.

Avery asked Newton, "Have you heard anything about Sebastian or the Favershams?"

He shook his head. "Nothing. There are no police reports that mention them, which is fortunate."

"Is the house still standing?" Reuben asked. He looked better than he had in days, and Avery presumed he'd finally had a good night's sleep.

"Yes, so they must have been able to limit the damage from Helena's attack."

"Good," Avery said, relieved. "I understand her vindictiveness, I even share it, but I can't condone murder."

"So what now?" El asked, finishing her last mouthful of pasta.

"We learn to master our new powers and spells," Alex said, grinning. "I still feel that magic we released flooding through me, although it has subsided a little."

Briar nodded. "Me, too. I sense a difference in the town, too. You see auras, Alex. Can you see the magic we released?"

"Sort of. It's like there's an extra energy to the place. I see it swirling in certain spots—I wandered up to All Souls earlier, it's certainly there—and there's definitely a cloud of energy over White Haven."

"So, what are the creatures Sebastian referred to?" Newton asked, worried. "Are they dangerous?"

"I've been thinking about that," El said. "I presume he meant more witches, and maybe spirits, too."

"I doubt Sebastian would have called witches 'creatures.' What about more demons?" Newton asked, rubbing his hands through his hair. "I have to think of the town and the surrounding area."

"Maybe," Briar said, glancing at the rest of them. "Maybe other things, like vampires or shape-shifters?"

"*Vampires?*" Avery asked, almost spitting out her wine. "Are you kidding?"

"Just because we've never seen one, doesn't mean they don't exist. After all, we'd never seen demons before. We sure know they exist now."

The table fell silent for a second, and then Avery sighed. "I might start researching, just in case."

"Well, if we've caused this problem," Newton began, and Avery smiled at the 'we,' "then it's our responsibility to manage it, and I expect every single one of you to do that." He looked around the table, meeting their gaze, one by one.

"Of course," Avery said, feeling the enormity of what might happen start to sink in.

"And Caspian, will he seek revenge?" Reuben asked.

"I doubt it," Alex said, sipping his beer thoughtfully. "Not yet, anyway, if at all. We defeated them last night. I think we're status quo now."

"I'd watch out for Helena, though," Briar said to Avery. "I think she'll stick around a while."

A knock interrupted their conversation, and Avery frowned. "I wonder who that is?" She pushed her chair back and headed to her front door, noting that Alex followed her to the top of the stairs.

Half the door was made of opaque glass, and she saw a tall figure on the other side. She opened the door warily, and found a woman standing outside. She was dressed in an elegant black dress, and her long, black hair was wound on top of her head in an elaborate chignon. She had been facing away, staring down the alley behind Avery's house, but as the door opened, she turned to face Avery, fixing her with a piercing glare of ice blue eyes. She was very striking, with high, angular cheekbones and dark red lips, full and expressive.

She was a witch.

"Good evening," the woman said, her voice low and compelling. Avery detected an Irish lilt to her accent. "My name is Genevieve Byrne. I am a member of the Witches Council, may I come in?"

For a second, Avery was speechless. Her grandmother had mentioned a Council; she thought it was just incoherent rambling, but apparently not.

Genevieve watched her, amusement mixed with annoyance on her face, and Avery finally found her tongue. "Of course, please come in."

She stepped back as Genevieve entered, bringing in a cloud of perfume.

Avery glanced up at Alex, who was watching with a frown on his face. "Follow me, Genevieve."

By the time they arrived in Avery's living room, everyone was standing, and Genevieve's gaze encompassed the room, as well as them.

Avery gave them all a meaningful glance. "Everyone, please meet Genevieve Byrne of the Witches Council."

"Good evening," Genevieve said in her low, lilting voice to the murmured greetings of the others. "I'm sorry to have interrupted you, but this is urgent."

"Not at all," Avery said, trying to subdue her worry and ignore the shocked faces of the others. "Please, take a seat."

She gestured to her sofa, and they all sat, on the floor or the sofa, watching their visitor.

Genevieve frowned. "I understood there were five witches, not six."

"I'm not a witch," Newton said, watching her as if she might bite. "I'm Detective Inspector Newton."

"Then you have no place here," Genevieve said haughtily.

"Yes, he does," Briar said immediately. "Anything you say to us, you can say to him."

"Really?" Genevieve said, fixing Briar with her inscrutable gaze. "I decide that, not you."

Avery was annoyed, and felt the wind begin to stir around her. "It's my house, and I say he stays. Go ahead, Genevieve."

"I will be brief," she said, looking at them dismissively. "Your actions yesterday were rash and ill-advised. You have angered the Council with your choices."

"What actions were they?" Avery asked, playing dumb.

"You know quite well what. You broke the seal beneath All Souls and allowed the magic contained within to pour forth. You may as well have lit a beacon on the hill by the castle. All manner of creatures will have sensed that power. The Council is greatly annoyed." She glared at each of them in turn.

"Never mind," Alex said, smoothly. "I'm sure you'll all get over it."

Avery suppressed a snigger, and then Briar spoke, an edge of annoyance in her tone. "To be quite honest, Genevieve, we didn't even know a Witches Council existed. Perhaps you should have introduced yourselves a little earlier. How on Earth were we to know this might be an issue? And to be quite honest, this is our families' magic we're talking about, so it really is no business of anyone else's."

Genevieve snapped. "Sebastian Faversham is dead because of you."

Reuben shouted, "You didn't seem to give much of a crap when my brother, Gil was murdered! Not important enough for your attention, you supercilious cow?"

Genevieve leapt to her feet, nose to nose with Reuben, who had stood now too, fists clenched at his side. "How dare you be so rude?"

"How dare you tell us what to do with our heritage?"

The tension shot up, and everyone stood.

Genevieve stepped back, her own hands also clenched, and Avery could feel her power resonating. She looked at them. "Your actions will have repercussions on the witch community. The Council meets in five days. One of you must attend to represent White Haven."

"Or else what?" Alex asked.

She sneered. "I suggest you take the opportunity to attend. Sebastian banned your membership for many years, as have many Favershams before him, but with Sebastian dead and the seal below All Souls gone, you now have an opportunity to sit on the Council and take part in real decisions about our magical community. You would do well to take advantage of it. With increased power comes increased responsibility. Don't miss your chance."

"And who takes Sebastian's place?" Avery asked, fearing she already knew the answer.

"Caspian, of course."

Genevieve headed to the stairs, ready to leave, but looked back at them. "Not many wished to have you on the Council, despite the recent events, but I fought for your place. It is only fitting, after you have been denied for centuries. Don't let me down. I will send word of the venue."

Avery followed her to the top of the steps, watching her as she descended. She vanished before she had even reached the bottom.

Avery turned back to the others, her heart pounding. The room had grown darker as the sun set, and shadows fell across the space, the candles glowing in dark corners and on table tops. Something monumental had occurred; they all knew it, and the relief from their sense of victory earlier in the evening had gone.

"What now?" Newton asked.

"Now we decide who's going to the Council," Avery said softly, her mind made up. "It seems we've been denied many things, for a very long time. I will not miss out again."

End of Book 2 of the White Haven Witches.
Magic Unleashed, White Haven Witches Book 3, is available to buy now.
Read on for an excerpt.

Thank you for reading *Magic Unbound*. All authors love reviews. They're important because they help drive sales and promotions, so I'd love it if you would leave a review. Scroll down the page to where it says, 'Write a customer review' and click. Thank you - your review is much appreciated.

MAGIC

WHITE HAVEN WITCHES (BOOK 3)

UNLEASHED

TJ GREEN

1

Avery stood on the cliff top looking out over White Haven harbour and the sea beyond. It was after ten at night and the moon peeked out behind ragged clouds, casting a milky white path over the water.

Alex stood next to her and sighed. "This is crazy. I told you it was a waste of time."

"We have to check. The old guy was insistent he'd seen something. He looked panic-stricken."

"He'd probably had a few too many rums."

"You didn't see him," Avery persisted. "He looked white, and he said he'd only seen something like it once before in his lifetime, and that was just before a couple of young men disappeared and were never seen again." Alex snorted, and Avery punched his arm. "I can't believe you're scoffing after all we've seen recently."

It had been just over a week since the five witches had broken the binding spell beneath the Church of All Souls, marking the end of a fight that had been going for centuries with the Favershams, a family of witches who lived in Harecombe, the town next to White Haven. The binding spell had been cast centuries earlier by Helena Marchmont, Avery's ancestor, and the other four witch families in White Haven. It had trapped a demon and the Faversham's ancestor beneath the church using a huge amount of magic. Breaking the spell had been difficult, but with the help of Helena's ghost they had succeeded, releasing magical energy that increased their own power. They had then defeated Sebastian Faversham, rescued Sally, and regained Reuben's missing grimoire. But Sebastian's final warning had proved correct. Strange things were indeed happening in White Haven.

In the last few days a dozen reports of strange noises and ghostly apparitions had been the centre of town gossip. Lights had appeared up at the ruined castle on the hill in the dead of night, and one fishing boat had reported seeing green lights in the depths of the sea, before they had hurriedly left the area and sailed for home.

On top of all that, Helena had reappeared, if only briefly, in Avery's flat. The scent of violets had manifested first, and then the smell of smoke and charred flesh, and Avery had yelled out, "*Helena! Stop it!*" Fortunately—or not, Avery couldn't work out which she preferred—she couldn't see Helena very often now, but it was unnerving to detect her unique presence in the flat. She hadn't resorted to warding the flat against her, but was seriously considering it.

Although Avery hoped these manifestations would settle down, she suspected they were only the beginning. And then that morning, an old man had appeared in the shop. He looked around nervously, and then approached Sally, who in turn escorted him over to Avery as she sorted some new stock in a quiet corner.

"This is Avery," Sally said cheerfully. "I'm sure she can help you, Caleb." She gave Avery a knowing look and left them to it, Caleb wringing his cap as if it was soaking wet.

"Hi Caleb, nice to meet you. How can I help?" Avery adopted her friendliest smile. Caleb looked as if she would bite. "I've, er, got something to tell you that you might find interestin'."

"Go on," she nodded encouragingly.

"I hear you may have abilities others may not," he said, almost stumbling over his words.

Oh, this was going to be one of those conversations.

She hesitated for a second, wondering what to say. "I may have, yes."

"I was on that fishing boat the other night."

Avery was confused for a second, and then realisation flashed across her brain. "The boat that saw the lights?" She looked at Caleb with renewed interest.

His hair was snowy white, but thick and brushed back from his face, falling to his collar. He had a full white beard, and wore a heavy blue jacket despite the heat, thick cotton trousers, and wellington boots. His face was covered in wrinkles, but his pale blue eyes were alert and watchful. He reminded her of the old sea captain from the fish fingers adverts.

"Yes, the boat that saw the lights. I wasn't going to say anything, but I remember only too well what happened the last time I saw them."

"You've seen them before?" Avery said, surprised. "Are you sure it wasn't just phosphorescence?"

"I know what that looks like, and this was different."

"Different how?" Avery asked, narrowing her eyes and feeling a shiver run through her.

"The lights circled below the boat, even and slow, three of them in all, and then started to weave a pattern below us. The young ones were transfixed. A wave crashed over the side and broke my concentration, but I could hear something." He stopped and looked away.

"What?" Avery insisted.

"Singing."

"Singing?"

"Strange, unearthly, hypnotic. I started the throttle and headed out of there, almost breaking our nets in the process."

Avery knew she should laugh at his outlandish suggestion, but she couldn't. He was so serious, and so absolutely believable. "And then what happened?"

"They disappeared. And I didn't look back."

"And the others?"

"Couldn't remember a thing."

"What happened the last time you saw them?"

"That was a very long time ago—I was only young myself." Caleb looked away again, shuffling uncomfortably, and then lowered his voice. "Young men disappeared. Vanished—*without a trace.*"

"But, how do you know that was related to the lights?" Avery felt bad for asking so many questions, but she half-wondered if he was winding her up.

"They'd been spotted with some young girls, and … Well, things weren't *normal.*"

Avery blinked and sighed. "I know I'm asking a lot of questions, Caleb, but why weren't they normal?"

"They were last seen at the beach, and their clothes were found there, but nothing else. And no, it wasn't suicide." He rushed on, clearly not wanting to be interrupted again. "I think they want something, I don't know why I think that, but I do. I *know* it. And it's only a matter of time before they arrive, so you need to stop them."

"How can I stop something I don't even know exists?" she asked, perplexed.

"I have no idea. I'm just offering you a warning." And with that he left the shop, leaving Avery looking after him, bewildered.

She sighed as she remembered her earlier conversation, and rubbed her head. "It sounds like it's out of a story book.

Mysterious lights in the sea, weird singing, loss of memory. Sebastian warned us that creatures would come. What if our magic sent a wave of power out into the sea? I guess it's possible."

Alex nodded, his features hard to see in the darkness on the cliff top. "The old myths talk of Sirens who sing sailors to their doom, but the old guy's story also reminds me a little of the Selkie myths."

"The seals that take human form?"

"Pretty much." He turned to her. "The myths haunt all coastal communities. They were popular in Ireland, particularly where I was on the west coast. And of course here in Cornwall there are Mermaid myths—they come looking for a man to take back to the sea with them to become their husbands and make lots of mer-babies."

"Great, so green lights and mysterious singing under the sea could be a rum-soaked hallucination, or maybe one of three weird myths."

He grinned. "Or a few others we haven't thought of, but I'll keep watch for women shrouded in seaweed or seal coats shed on the beach."

"You're so funny, Alex," she said, thinking the complete opposite.

He turned to her and pulled her into his arms. "I don't care how alluring they're supposed to be, they wouldn't be half as alluring as you."

She put her hands against his chest, feeling the strong beat of his heart and the warmth of his skin through his t-shirt, and looked up into his warm brown eyes. She could feel her own pulse starting to flutter wildly and wondered if he realised quite what he did to her. "You're very alluring yourself."

"How alluring?" he asked, his lips a feather-light touch on her neck.

"Too alluring." She could feel a tingle of desire running through her from their contact.

"No such thing," he said softly. His hand caressed the back of her neck and pulled her close for a long, deep kiss as his hands tangled in her hair. Pulled so close to him, she felt his desire start to grow, and he stepped away, a wicked gleam in his eyes. "Let's go back to mine. I've got better things in mind than standing on a cliff top."

***

However, when they arrived at Alex's pub, The Wayward Son, Newton was at the bar, sipping a pint of beer.

Mathias Newton was a Detective Inspector with the Cornwall Police, who also knew that they were witches. His history was as complicated as theirs, and although their relationship had started badly, they were now friends. He turned from where he'd been scowling into his pint, half an eye on the football highlights that were on the muted TV screen in the corner, and half an eye on the door. He was in casual clothing, his short dark hair slightly ruffled, and his grey eyes were serious. "Where have you two been?"

"Nice to see you, too," Avery greeted him. She slid onto the seat next to him while Alex leaned on the bar and ordered the drinks.

Alex groaned. "Your timing sucks, Newton. I had better things in mind than a pint."

He just grunted. "Get over it."

"You look as grumpy as hell," Avery said.

"That's because I am. We've had some odd reports at the station."

Avery felt her heart sink. *Not more strange things.* "Like what?"

"Odd disturbances—noises at night, people thinking they're being broken into, electrical shorts, missing items, but no signs of a break-in."

Alex raised an eyebrow and passed Avery a glass of red wine. "People report electrical shorts to you?"

"You'd be surprised what people report to us. But yes. We've had a flood of reports over the last couple of days. I wanted to know if you've seen anything."

"Lots of rumours of weird happenings, but nothing concrete." She related the story the old sailor, Caleb, had told her. "We've been up on the cliff top to see if we could spot anything, but..." She shrugged.

Newton rubbed his hand through his hair, ruffling it even more. "I'd hoped things would go back to normal after the other night, but they're really not. Briar and Elspeth have both had people coming into their shop sharing strange tales, and Elspeth has been selling lots of protection charms."

"Really?" Avery asked. "I must admit, I haven't spoken to them in a couple of days."

"It's my job to, Avery." He finished his pint and ordered another. "Have you heard about the meeting?" Newton was referring to the Witches Council.

She nodded. "Yes. It's tomorrow evening, at eight."

To celebrate defeating the Favershams and breaking the binding spell, they had all met for dinner at Avery's flat, but it had been interrupted by the arrival of Genevieve Byrne, another witch who organised the Witches Council, a group they hadn't even known existed until that night. She had invited them to the next meeting, actually almost insisted that they attend, and after that their celebrations had taken a downward turn as they each debated the merits of whether to go or not. For Avery, it was an easy decision. They'd been invited to something they'd been excluded from for years, and she had no intention of letting the opportunity pass her by.

Reuben had not felt the same. "Screw them all, why the hell should we go to their crappy meeting?"

"Because we'll learn something, Reuben," Avery had answered, exasperated. "Aren't you the slightest bit interested in knowing who they are and what they do?"

"No," he'd answered belligerently.

"Well, I am," Briar said. "But I'm too chicken to go."

"I'm not sure I trust her or any of them," Newton said, "but maybe that's the policeman in me."

Alex had nodded in agreement. "I don't entirely trust them either, but I agree with Avery and Briar. We should go. We need to have a stake in whatever's going on around here."

"Well, unless anyone else really wants to go, I'd love to go first," Avery said. "Someone else can go next time."

Alex rolled his eyes. "Just when I thought things might start to get back to normal around here."

But at least most of them had agreed on attending.

However, now, in the warm comfort of the pub, Avery felt a bit worried about going and the reception she might receive. The other night beneath All Souls now felt like a dream—if it hadn't been for the headlines that proclaimed the death of Sebastian Faversham in an electrical fire at the family home. A fake report. He had actually died after being attacked by Helena's ghost, her spirit made stronger by the extra surge of magical energy that pulsed through her like a bolt of lightning.

"Where?" Newton persisted, drawing her back to the present.

"Some place called Crag's End."

"Where the hell's that?"

"Around Mevagissey, somewhere just off the coast. It seems to be a very large, private residence."

He looked concerned. "I'm not sure you should go alone."

"That's what I said," Alex agreed, gazing at Avery.

Avery twisted to look up at him. "Alex, I'll be fine. They're all witches, I'm sure I'll be quite safe."

"We don't know any of them."

"We were invited. Stop worrying," she said, as much to reassure herself as him.

"Someone should go with you," Newton said.

Avery looked between the two of them. "Something is very wrong with the world when the two of you start agreeing. No. I'm going alone. Trust me. I'm a witch."

Author's Note

Thank you for reading *Magic Unbound,* the second book in the White Haven Witches series.

I really enjoyed fleshing out more of my characters' back stories and growing their universe, and I'm already working hard on book 3, *Magic Unleashed.* Their lives aren't going to get any easier, and in fact, they're going to get a lot busier! I can't wait to share the fun, and I'm aiming to release by March 2019.

Thanks again to Fiona Jayde Media for my awesome cover, and thanks to Kyla Stein at Missed Period Editing for tidying up my draft.

Thanks also to my beta readers, glad you enjoyed it, your feedback as ever is very helpful!

Thanks also to my launch team, who give valuable feedback on typos and are happy to review on release. It's lovely to hear from them - you know who you are - and their feedback is always so encouraging. I'm lucky to have them on my team! I love hearing from all my readers, so I welcome you to get in touch.

If you'd like to read a bit more background to the stories, please head to my website, www.tjgreen.nz, where I'll be blogging about the books I've read and the research I've done on the series - in fact there's lots of stuff on there about my other series, Tom's Arthurian Legacy, too.

If you'd like to read more of my writing, please join my mailing list by visiting my website - www.tjgreen.nz. You can get a free short story called *Jack's Encounter*, describing how Jack met Fahey – a longer version of the prologue in *Tom's Inheritance* – by subscribing to my newsletter. You'll also get a FREE copy of *Excalibur Rises*, a short story prequel.

You will also receive free character sheets on all of my main characters in White Haven Witches - exclusive to my email list!

By staying on my mailing list you'll receive free excerpts of my new books, as well as short stories and news of giveaways. I'll also be sharing information about other books in this genre you might enjoy.

I look forward to you joining my readers' group.

About the Author

I grew up in England and now live in the Hutt Valley, near Wellington, New Zealand, with my partner Jason, and my cats Sacha and Leia. When I'm not writing, you'll find me with my head in a book, gardening, or doing yoga. And maybe getting some retail therapy!

In a previous life I've been a singer in a band, and have done some acting with a theatre company – both of which were lots of fun. On occasions I make short films with a few friends, which begs the question, where are the book trailers? Thinking on it ...

I'm currently working on more books in the White Haven Witches series, musing on a prequel, and planning for a fourth book in Tom's Arthurian Legacy series.

Please follow me on social media to keep up to date with my news, or join my mailing list - I promise I don't spam! Join my mailing list by visiting www.tjgreen.nz.

You can follow me on social media -

Website: http://www.tjgreen.nz
Facebook: https://www.facebook.com/tjgreenauthor/
Twitter: https://twitter.com/tjay_green
Pinterest:
https://nz.pinterest.com/mount0live/my-books-and-writing/

Goodreads:
https://www.goodreads.com/author/show/15099365.T_J_Green
Instagram:
https://www.instagram.com/mountolivepublishing/
BookBub: https://www.bookbub.com/authors/tj-green
Amazon:
https://www.amazon.com/TJ-Green/e/B01D7V8LJK/